The Masquerade of Istanbul

Mehmet Agop

To Occam's Razor:

Choose the simpler one.

Contents

1

At the Airport

The moment Fehmi saw Mary Heather at the Istanbul Atatürk Airport something in him stirred.

Mary Heather was his brother Rafet's American wife. She was visiting Turkey for the first time. The year was 1998. It was summer. The brothers' father had passed away a couple of months ago and they had to sort out the inheritance. Rafet was also going to use this break to do his compulsory short-term military service.

Fehmi himself was a father of two – two teenage daughters. He was a quiet man, smaller than average, neatly dressed in formal trousers and a plain shirt. Everyone who knew him pointed out that he was on the conservative side; 'A bit religious,' they whispered.

That day Mary Heather was wearing a simple white blouse, blue linen trousers and flip-flops. Her toenails were painted red. Her long blonde hair and white skin were shining as brightly as the summer sun outside. She was slightly overweight but in a nice, tidy way. The whole family were happy to be meeting the relatives from abroad, especially her, and no one noticed how intently Fehmi's eyes lingered on her... on her eyes, her

1

nose, her shoulders, her hands… before his gaze shifted to her feet, to her second toe that was longer than the big one…

Part 1

Mehmet Agop

2

Resemblance

Fehmi Aslan was born in 1958 and grew up in a westernised family in Istanbul.

His father Kemal Bey owned a clothing store in the Old City. He was a staunchly secular man. Every working day he proudly put on a three-piece suit and tie; he taught his wife to wear modern clothes; he celebrated special days by drinking red wine. Never in his life did he fail to vote. On election days he dressed his two sons smartly and took them along to the polling station to vote for the Republican People's Party, the left-wing secular party founded by Atatürk. He believed that religious parties had no right to exist. He avoided mosques and argued that religions were philosophies that were incompatible with science.

There were no incidents in Fehmi's early years that could explain his actions as an adult. Nor were there any signs that he might do such things. He was quiet, yes – and quietness is a mysterious trait. But otherwise he was a successful student; no one bullied him, he didn't bully anyone. Despite his short stature, there was an aura about him that kept the big boys away, that

5

made them spare him each time. 'You are a good boy!' they would say.

For his university education Fehmi went to Ankara, to experience living away from home. In line with his father's wishes, he signed up for a Management degree – though he was less certain whether he would subsequently want to take over the clothing store.

In the first few months he regretted going to Ankara. He had to share a small dormitory room cluttered with bunk beds, a table and four chairs with seven other people. His roommates, all from boarding schools, were terribly accustomed to throwing their dirty underwear on the floor and leaving bits of feta cheese and breadcrumbs on the table. The smell of the room, Fehmi complained, was worse than the foot odour in mosques after the Friday prayers.

Sometimes they borrowed his razor handle without his permission or slept in his bed at the weekends he travelled to Istanbul. Fehmi Aslan devised delicate techniques to deal with these. He bought a second razor which he kept visible in his wardrobe, hiding away the main one. And before he went away for the weekend, he removed his bed sheets on the pretext that they had to be washed.

In the morning, whilst everyone was still in bed, the cleaner stepped in with his besom but without a dustpan, stirring up the dust and waking them. Once he had left, they all went back to sleep, for nights revolved around card games and drinking.

Initially, Fehmi attempted to isolate himself, studying

regularly, going to bed early, sleeping using earplugs. But exams didn't go well and, after the first results were announced, he gave up studying.

He joined in the games, drank *rakı* and gossiped in the dorm hallway. It was in the hallway that Hakan Yavuz initiated him into smoking and politics. Hakan was a leftist, as were most of the students in that grey dormitory block. In principle Fehmi liked communism, but he was too individualistic to be an active member of any group.

And that day, the day he met Jale, it was solely out of curiosity that he agreed to participate in the protest against the rise in prices at the university cafeteria.

Jale was in the very front of the group with three other girls. Whereas majority of the people were shuffling along and perfunctorily clapping their hands, the girls in the front were full of energy. They shouted slogans with passion. They cheered on the group. Above their heads they carried placards.

Noticing Jale, Hakan dragged Fehmi and they strode two paces behind her for the rest of the march. Then, in front of the rector's office, they were the ones who sang the monotonous *türkü* the loudest. And finally, at the end, when the group was dispersing, Hakan introduced Fehmi to her.

Her blonde wavy hair was tied in a ponytail. She was a well-built, lusty girl. She had a little bit of excess weight around her midriff and hips, a beautiful feminine weight, the type of weight that turns a girl into a woman and without which she would have looked incomplete.

Hakan had gone out with her a number of times, insisting on paying the bills at the restaurants, though had been unable to go a step beyond. Jale hadn't said anything negative; but she had not encouraged him either. It was as if she wished him to just hang around and Hakan was willing to do so, hoping that one day he might be able to persuade her.

Hakan was not surprised that after they left Fehmi could not stop talking about Jale. Fehmi was intrigued that a girl from a rich background would take part in a leftist event. Unlike the other girls in that group who seemed to associate unkemptness with being communist, Jale was stylishly dressed in a black miniskirt and see-through stockings. Her nails were manicured and painted burgundy. 'She smokes so sexily you could watch her smoking all day,' Fehmi was saying.

Hakan Yavuz was well aware how attractive Jale was and normally he would have tolerated his friend's excitement. But that day something in Jale's demeanour towards Fehmi had caught his attention. Hence, as they were parting, he felt the need to warn him off.

'It's wrong,' he said firmly, 'for a man to court a girl his friend is interested in.'

The next day, finding himself musing about Jale, Hakan Yavuz's words weighed heavily on Fehmi's conscience. He went on a long walk to the central park, his hands in the pockets of his charcoal coat. Every now and again he paused to gaze at the trees, the pigeons, the fountains. He picked up leaves off the ground, tearing them into tiny pieces. If you know what you want to do, then why worry? Where had he come across this expression, who had told him, he could not remember. But by the evening he decided that there were times in life when one had to be selfish.

Before he went to Jale, over lunch, he informed Hakan of his intention.

Hakan Yavuz's reply was curt: 'Your choice,' he said, staring out of the window. 'This means this is my last lunch with you.'

When Fehmi asked Jale out for a movie and she accepted, no one except Hakan predicted anything further would develop between them; they merely considered him to be another one of her victims who would suffer from unrequited love. Nevertheless, boys from the neighbouring dormitory rooms, hearing the gossip, rushed over to inquire and condescendingly pat Fehmi on the back. 'Well done! Good job!' they said.

They were baffled by the mismatch; that Fehmi, a small boy, could even go out once with a girl as strong as Jale.

It was a riddle.

After that first date, Fehmi and Jale were always seen together on the campus. But never did they hold hands, nor make any other physical contact. This left people wondering about the nature of their relationship. When quizzed over it Fehmi referred to her as his girlfriend. Privately, however, he was frustrated, unsure of what his next move should be. Jale was behind a closed door and he was waiting in front of it for her to open it. He was afraid of making a mistake and losing her.

He made her interests his own. He devoured books on communism he found in the library. Jale admired Lenin, and Fehmi specifically memorised anecdotes from Lenin's life so that he did not run out of things to tell her. They went to communist meetings, cafés, plays, concerts he would not have ordinarily gone to. *I'm learning how to be with a girl*, Fehmi was thinking. Yet, he had not even held her hand.

About four months later, one Friday night after drinking in a cheap bar in Kızılay, Jale took him to the flat she was sharing with two other girls. Sitting on her bed, they kissed. Then Jale shifted herself forward, brushing her breasts against him. Fehmi's heart was beating wildly. He was still debating whether to touch her or not. Jale eventually had to take his hand and place it on her breast. It was at that point that Fehmi gained courage and slid his hand under her sweater, later taking it off, along with her navy blue lace bra.

Fehmi Aslan had never laid eyes on a naked girl before, and the way he hovered over her huge, firm breasts, as though he were imprinting the shape of them on his mind, put a smile on Jale's face. She went as far as caressing his penis but not unzipping his bell-bottoms. She suddenly stopped him after a while, by pushing his hand away. Then she covered herself with sheets and they lay on their backs side by side without saying anything.

The next couple of weeks were the happiest time of Fehmi's life. He described that night in detail to his friends. Despite the sadness of losing Hakan's friendship, he was gratified to be the winner; it was marvellous to be with a girl his once best friend adored.

It became their custom to drink and then end up at her home on Fridays. But each time Jale prevented him from going any further. Her roughness confounded and even offended him. She would grasp his wrist, or shove him off, or pull her top down. And then they would lie quietly. At times like that she seemed so distant it was as if making love reminded her of something horrible.

Sometimes she broke the silence and told things about herself. When she was fifteen, she met her first boyfriend who was a university student. She was at an American boarding school in Istanbul at the time, and would compose a fake letter so that she could leave the dorm and be with him at the weekends. They were together for two years. 'What happened in the end?' Fehmi asked once, but Jale didn't reply.

After she fell asleep, Fehmi would slip on his clothes and tiptoe out of the flat.

In public Jale was still avoiding physical contact, being careful about the impression they gave. This, though, was a minor matter which Fehmi was willing to overlook. He was convinced they were now in a relationship and he was looking forward to each new day.

In the library he surreptitiously scoured biology encyclopaedias, to fill in the gaps in his knowledge, to be prepared if the opportunity arose. For more practical knowledge he went to the sex movies.

In those years of political instability (from '72 to '80

there were nine different governments, all of which were coalitions or minorities), with the communists and fascists fighting on the streets, and the economy crumbling to an extent such that queues formed outside shops when oil and sugar were available, the sex cinemas were havens where people could have a respite from their everyday miseries. As a result, the Turkish sex film industry was one of the few booming sectors. In 1972 alone a total of 294 films were made. A leading actress, in just one year, in 1979, appeared in 37 films. The efforts to keep up with the demand gave rise to stories that directors filmed two movies at once, using scenarios jotted on cigarette packs. A bedroom and a handful of men and women were sufficient for most of the scenes.

What started off as erotic films in the early seventies, by the end of the decade neared porn with a heavy dose of comedy. Watching those absurd creations in which actors chased each other in a house and pretended to have sex whilst their white cotton undergarments were visible on the screen, Fehmi dreamed of what was going to happen next with Jale.

Then days turned into weeks, weeks into months, but Jale did not invite him to her flat again. Whenever he inquired about it, she produced an excuse. Fehmi went over every moment, searching for where he had gone wrong. The feeling that he was sitting in front of her door, waiting for her to open it, returned. And, eventually, he was unable to stop himself from murmuring his frustration to his friends.

He never phrased it clearly. Each complaint was seemingly unconnected to the others. He once said he was having doubts about whether she was the right girl for him. On another occasion he revealed that she had a problem from the past that he had not been able to unearth. 'I even took her out to the best restaurant in town. Yet no progress,' he moaned at one time.

Fehmi could guess that the boys in the dormitory were suspecting he was concealing something and that they were ridiculing him behind his back, pointing out that their initial judgements that Jale was too good for him were justified.

In those days, Fehmi gave up shaving. He lost his enthusiasm for communist activities. He became more introverted, more philosophical about life. Staring at his pile of bland textbooks, he questioned whether he should continue with Management or switch to a course that would provide him with tangible skills, skills that would enable him to be less dependent on other people.

He needed an inspiration, something to which he could divert his energy. Perhaps he could have taken up a sport – tennis or basketball. Or perhaps he should have broken it off with Jale and tried to move on.

Then, one evening, on his way back to the dormitory, in an alleyway across the road he saw two boys from the neighbouring room shot dead. It occurred so abruptly, so unexpectedly that he could barely perceive it. The gunmen ran away on foot before Fehmi could even hide behind the cars. As he rushed past the alley to his dormitory block, he caught sight of the blood splattered on the wall and the graffiti that said *Fascist Communist* in black letters. Shivering, from a window on the fourth floor, he observed the crowd gathering and the police and ambulance arriving.

Four days later they were lined up in the courtyard of a mosque for the funeral prayers. There was an altercation at the beginning over whether women should be praying at the back or whether they could be positioned next to the men, with the Imam quoting from the Koran to support his stance. But Fehmi didn't even understand what the issue was. Being so close to the coffins of his friends had distanced him from the world around him. As far as he was aware, they both were the type of people who read about communism in books and would never pick up a gun. He could not help thinking that this could have been his funeral.

Fehmi had never prayed in his life until then; he didn't know how to pray. Therefore, he followed the people around him, bending down and standing up as they did.

At one stage, when he had prostrated himself, he felt alone in the crowd. His mind flashed back to that evening. He wondered whether the *Fascist Communist* graffiti manifested the ignorance of its authors or whether it showed how much a political ideology that was supposed to be humanistic had gone astray in the hands of ordinary people. What took place in practice, in countries like the Soviet Union, had so little to do with Marxism; people would never be enlightened and responsible enough for Marxism to be viable.

He was reflecting on how pointless it was to die for

such a cause when he lifted his head up and noticed that the people around him were already on their feet. They were almost finished with their prayers.

That day, as Fehmi and Jale were leaving the mosque, they ran into Hakan Yavuz. Hakan had not spoken to Fehmi since his last lunch with him, and he hardly greeted him. As usual Jale was friendly with Hakan. Twice, 'Let's go,' Fehmi said, interrupting them, but she failed to respond.

Fehmi was taciturn in the subsequent days. When Jale asked what was bothering him, he said, 'If not killed on the streets, we are going to rot in the prison.' He claimed that communists in Turkey were fighting a lost battle. It could not be more obvious who the state was siding with: communist legends were either martyrs or in prison, but the fascist ones were alive, on the run, miraculously escaping arrest at the last minute!

A week later Fehmi went back to the mosque – this time on his own.

He sat on the carpet with his back to a pillar, relishing the silence. Shortly after, when the midday prayers commenced, he joined in. He found praying, the physical aspect of it, the harmony of the group, the togetherness to be soothing. He could forget about the riots, the unrest, the dysfunctional government, and, most importantly, about his troubles with Jale.

That day he resolved to go to the mosque more often.

In the following months, especially at night, the streets grew more dangerous. Gunshots were so common they ceased to startle people; even cats learned not to react. In

October 1978, seven leftist students watching television in a Bahçelievler flat in central Ankara were brutally murdered by fascists. The Alawite Muslim (leftist) - Sunni Muslim (rightist) conflicts in December, in the eastern city of Kahramanmaraş, during which over 100 people died, illustrated that the division of left and right was no longer merely political but had metastasised like a malignant form of cancer.

The police and army were doing little to quell the disturbances, as if they were allowing grounds to be established for a coup d'état (which would happen in 1980). The university was frequently shut down due to incidents on the campus and Fehmi was spending his time in bed reading novels, sometimes not taking a shower for ten days at a stretch. Occasionally he went out to pray or meet up with Jale. Once she even took him to her flat and made love like mad. But it pained Fehmi; it only served to show the level of control she had over him; that he was a slave who worshiped his master.

Then one afternoon, as he was coming out of the cafeteria, he saw her kissing a boy quite a few years older than her. He immediately realised who he was, and he was astonished by how much he resembled him.

The next day Fehmi Aslan packed his bags and, without informing anyone, left Ankara.

3

Watching the River

Precisely three months after his return to Istanbul, Fehmi was married.

'I'm not going to do anything for a while. I want to get out of the river that life is and watch it,' he had told his parents upon his arrival.

To them it sounded like a joke, an unheard of luxury. They nagged at him day after day, asking what his plans were, implying that he could not just sit at home and do nothing.

He tried to avoid them, locking himself in his bedroom in that Galata flat, emerging only to eat. During the day he went on long walks.

It was the Old City – which he could see from his bedroom window – that intrigued him most. As if it held the answer in its jumble of buildings and narrow alleys. He did not know what he was searching for, whether it was another human being or a hidden café or a mysterious organisation, but every day he strode all the way down from the Genoese Galata Tower to the Golden Horn and then crossed over the bridge into the Old City.

In the Old City he passed through bazaars, explored cisterns, discovered caravanserais converted into malls, sneaked into abandoned wooden houses. One day, at a point when he was totally lost, in a busy lane of clothing shops, he stumbled upon a narrow doorway. The off-white stones indicated it was an Ottoman structure. There were no signs on it, nothing on the outside to suggest what it might be, and that was what impelled him to go up the flight of stone stairs.

On the landing he paused to look through the iron grated window. Down below was a tiny square where pedlars were sitting on the ground selling goods they had laid on jute sacks. It was a timeless scene, a scene that probably had not changed for centuries. The next set of stairs took him into the courtyard of a mosque. The immediate tranquillity up there, the way it felt so removed from the noisy streets, that such a secluded place could exist in such a busy part of the city struck him as magical. And when he entered the mosque and beheld the tiles that were more magnificent, more ornate than any other in the city, he was certain that this place, the 16th century Rüstem Paşa Mosque, would be his secret garden.

In the coming weeks, day after day, Fehmi went to that mosque. After leaving Ankara, even though religion had been on his mind, he hadn't prayed. And so it was in that mosque that he began to pray again. But most of his time in there was devoted to gazing at the blue and white tiles, and contemplating. Contemplating the meaning of life and what to do with himself.

The anarchy that had taken over the country, the gunshots that woke him up at night were things he could not relate to. Going to university in such circumstances was a waste of his time. Nor did he wish to be anywhere near Jale. He yearned for something light, something straightforward. Then one afternoon, when his eyes were fixed on a floral tile that was different from all the others around it, the hypothesis that would haunt him for the rest of his life occurred to him.

The hypothesis was simple: there was nothing such as a calling or destiny. Therefore, there were several possibilities open to him and it was solely up to him to choose any one of those. For instance, he could remain single and roam from one country to another, doing random work. Or he could take up a nine-to-five job, marry and have children. Or he could put off marriage until he was 40, venture into business, and dedicate himself to achieving financial security. In each of these possibilities he saw a version of Fehmi Aslan. A businessman, a family man, an adventurer…

All he had to do was to select one and then he could shape himself into that personality.

As his attendance at the five daily prayers became more regular, Fehmi came to associate the serenity of the Rüstem Paşa Mosque with religion itself. Religion, he reasoned, could form a basis on which he could build his life. It was in that frame of mind, during a period he thought he could not put up with living in the same place as his parents any more, that Fehmi decided he was going to marry, settle down, and work with his father in the clothing store.

His father Kemal Bey was utterly dismayed by what he heard and tried hard to dissuade him. He even told him not to rush, that he could take his time. Kemal Bey dearly wanted his two sons to be university graduates. He did not have unrealistic expectations of them. In any case, he had set up the business with the view that they would take it over one day, but he dreamed of hanging their university diplomas on the wall in the office at the back of the store and pointing at them when people visited.

Conceding that Fehmi was not going to budge, around that time Kemal Bey resolved to send his younger son Rafet to a university in America. Financially it was not going to be easy. But at least one of his sons would have the opportunity to be away from the turmoil and study.

**

Tülin, the bride, was from the same neighbourhood, a 17-year old high school dropout. Fehmi was acquainted with her since childhood. In their teenage years they had often had friendly conversations on the street whilst they were within a larger group. But they hadn't had a period of flirtation as such. Fehmi chose her on a whim. So once his mother had completed her inquiries with regard to her family, his parents reluctantly went to formally ask for her hand.

Her family were migrants from the south-eastern

town of Mardin. They dwelled in one of the more modest apartments down the hill. Her father worked as a minibus driver for a wealthy relative; her mother was a housewife. Tülin herself was attending a tailoring course at the time. Even when she was growing up she had the attitude of a spinster waiting for a husband. She was an unassuming girl who had a clear perception of what her role in the family would be. She was skilled in cooking and housekeeping. She presumed that her husband would be the breadwinner and accepted that whatever he said had to be obeyed.

Her parents deemed Fehmi to be a good prospect and Tülin, too, consented.

Back then, Tülin did not wear a headscarf and her wedding dress was tight-fitting with a moderate neckline. Even her mother who in everyday life covered her head with a flowery scarf opted not to on the wedding day. When years later their daughters Merve and Seher picked up the framed photograph of the modern-looking couple, they were astounded by how much their parents had deviated from that starting point, by how they could have deviated so much.

After the wedding, the couple moved into a nearby flat Fehmi's father grumblingly bought for them and Fehmi set out on a life split between home and work. He prayed regularly, and in his spare time he read poorly-written books interpreting the Koran. He was charmed by the plainness of his new life.

Spurred on by his studies, one evening two months later, Fehmi Aslan broached the subject of headscarf with the new bride. He said that she was so chaste that he would be happy if she were to keep herself for his eyes only. There was no mention of the religious aspect of it. And Tülin, the girl who had been waiting for a husband to give her life a direction, acquiesced.

It is likely that even if Fehmi had not requested, Tülin would have put on a headscarf later in life. In her family virtually all women did; it was a social norm that after a certain age a woman loosely wrapped a scarf around her head before she went out. For her it was a symbol of an honourable married woman rather than a religious one.

Then, as years went by, Fehmi's interest in religion waned. Even from what they observed, even from what they could deduce – without being aware of the full extent of his deeds, of what he had detected with his Soviet binoculars, of the former communists and the high heels, of the drawn curtains and the encounter on the stairs, of the bikinis and lingerie – his family could tell that he was not the person he used to be. First, he began to skip his daily prayers. Then quite how or why they did not know, they could no longer recall when exactly, he took up drinking again. He did not drink much though. Just once in a while he arrived home smelling of *rakı*.

There was even an instance where he forced his wife to wear a miniskirt and bikini for the first time in her life whilst they were on holiday in the Mediterranean (although by then it had been more than ten years since Tülin had last gone out with her head uncovered). The decision to travel had come completely out of the blue.

And the way Fehmi behaved over those ten days shocked and disconcerted Tülin. It was as if he had become unhinged. She never understood his objective and nothing followed it. From her point of view, it was a bizarre one-off incident. For a while she didn't tell anyone about it and when she eventually broke her silence one afternoon to whisper it to the next-door neighbour she was still in awe of what had taken place.

Other than that one time they did not go on holiday. This was not due to economic constraints: it was out of choice. Fehmi preferred to stay at home in the summers, and feasts were celebrated with the extended family.

Despite these conspicuous aberrations, Fehmi never entirely gave up religion. Perhaps it provided him with an anchor, a point to return to. To counter the unbearable lightness of life. Or maybe because he had already gone a long way down that route and he couldn't turn back. Whatever the reason, religion always remained a part of Fehmi Aslan.

Every Feast of Sacrifice a sheep was slaughtered. He fasted during the holy month of Ramadan. The summer Merve was thirteen and Seher ten they were both sent to the Koran course for the neighbourhood children at the 14th century Arab Mosque.

He was strict with the clothes his daughters wore. Arms and legs had to be concealed; curves unidentifiable. Even at school, a private institution where most students were from secular families and girls wore short skirts (as short as the teachers tolerated), Merve and Seher had to wear absurdly bulky skirts. When he learned that girls were supposed to put on tights in Physical Education classes, Fehmi obtained sick notes from a doctor who was a family friend so his daughters could be exempt.

Throughout those years, he continued to work with his father at the clothing store in the Old City. Kemal Bey was disturbed by his son's religiousness. This was not how he had desired him to be. Fehmi should have taken a step further than he had towards being westernised. Fehmi's daughters should have learned the violin or the piano; should have had the culture to appreciate opera.

In the store they sold all kinds of women's garments, formal and casual, including swimming costumes. Except for the bikinis, all items were modest. Skirts not very short, necklines not very low. It was a store for schoolteachers and civil servants – for the typical modern lady of the Republic that Atatürk had envisaged.

It was only in his latter years, as a reaction against the rise of political Islam and to provoke his son, that Kemal Bey grew more attached to bikinis.

Those were the days when the discussions about the secularism of the state were reduced to bikinis and headscarves. The nation had polarized, with the defenders of the bikini lined up against the defenders of the headscarf.

The Headscarf People querying why doctors, civil servants, MPs, teachers, students were not permitted to wear headscarves, with the Bikini People defending the dress code, indicating that a woman couldn't go to school, parliament, university, hospital, mosque in a bikini either. The Headscarf People complaining that the Bikini People were being undemocratic; the Bikini People in turn accusing them of nurturing a hidden fundamentalist agenda. At state receptions the Bikini People ostentatiously drank champagne, whilst the Headscarf People demanded fruit juice to be put in their wine glasses.

By the mid-'90s, with the religious Welfare Party gaining ground, the balance had tipped in favour of the Headscarf People. The Headscarf People, who had been the underdogs since the secular republic had been established seventy years ago, were now imposing their views on the Bikini People. In the WP municipalities it was a struggle to find a restaurant that served *rakı*; nudist artworks were censored; ladies in bikinis were harassed by bearded men on beaches.

Kemal Bey argued that the bikini represented progress, that the bikini distinguished Turkey from the rest of the Muslim world. When the WP won the 1994 municipality elections in Istanbul – the first time in history that a religious party had – he dressed all of the six window dummies in the shop in red bikinis. As though the bikini were the RPP flag. Every morning when they opened the store, the dummies in bikinis greeted them. Fehmi was naturally annoyed by this. But Kemal Bey was adamant: 'You'll have to wait until my death to remove these,' he told Fehmi.

It also bothered Kemal Bey that newspapers had moved their offices from the nearby Babı-Ali to the outskirts of the city. Journalism had been a castle of secularism in the Old City. His hope was that tourism would rescue this area from the hands of the fundamentalists. At the same time, he was aware that there was not much else he could do: his health was deteriorating and he would have no control over what would happen after his death. His generation was passing. And Fehmi knew this too. So he took to biding his time, allowing his father to do as he wished, as the store fell into disrepair and stock was left lying around.

It was in the spring of 1998 that Kemal Bey passed away. He worked up to a month before his death. Every day smartly dressed in a three-piece suit.

Part 2

Mehmet Agop

4

Holiday in Turkey

Then, in the summer of 1998, Fehmi's brother Rafet came from America to resolve the inheritance issues and to do his one-month military service.

Rafet had missed his father's funeral due to his anxiety over his job. For more than two years the company he was working for had been experiencing financial difficulties. Departments had already been restructured twice and rumours about what might happen next had intensified. In such circumstances it had not felt appropriate to request compassionate leave, especially given that he would have to take a long-haul flight and be off for a full week.

On this trip with him were his American wife Mary Heather and their two children who were visiting Turkey for the first time. Rafet himself had last been back for two weeks in the eighties when his mother was undergoing an appendicitis operation. In those years he was satisfied with his life in America and, during that fortnight, he was happy to talk to the extended family and neighbours about his house in the suburbs of Pittsburgh, his two cars and his job at a multinational company. They were eager to find out about his salary and so he detailed his contract. 'Extra benefits, too. Health insurance, private pension scheme, lump sums.' He commiserated with them that life indeed was tough in Turkey; they were lucky if they could make ends meet. Having only worked with his father and never left Istanbul since his return from university, Fehmi was disturbed by all the attention his younger brother was receiving. And the sole way he was able to cope with this was by staying away and going on long walks.

This time, however, Rafet was not keen to talk about his job or divulge his income. He didn't even mention that he had been promoted barely eighteen months ago. In him there was no trace of the ambitious ladder-climber of the corporate business world. The smirk on his face had faded away.

In the presence of his mother and neighbours he glossed over his work status. But in private to Fehmi he spoke about the layoffs made lately. He complained that there were very few vacancies at his level, progression was not easy, performance alone was not sufficient, networking counted more. Particularly, becoming a manager as a foreigner was impossible, he claimed.

The brothers spent that first month – the month before Rafet left for his military service – almost exclusively in each other's company. They went out on strolls, called at the clothing store, sat together on the balcony in the evenings. On a couple of occasions Rafet took his family out on dinner, introducing them to the various types of kebabs.

Apart from those days, Mary Heather remained indoors. She had no real interest in exploring a new city. Until this summer her life had taken place in three locations: Pennsylvania (where she resided), Florida (where her mother had moved to three years ago), and New York City (where she had had a weekend with Rafet at the age of 23). She had not been out of the USA before. No one in her family had except an uncle who had served in a military base in Japan. It was for this trip that she had obtained her first ever passport.

As neither Tülin nor Grandmother spoke English, her communication with them was through hand gestures and irritating smiles. Sometimes she talked to the two teenage daughters, Seher and Merve. But they mostly preferred to entertain their cousins, practising their English, teaching them Turkish.

So whilst Rafet was away on his duty, Fehmi was the only adult with whom she could have a reasonable conversation. From the time Fehmi had seen Mary Heather at the Atatürk Airport something in him had stirred. He was amazed that this blonde foreign lady with painted toenails, wearing flip-flops and simple clothes, could be his brother's wife, that she was part of the family.

He could not stop himself from comparing her to his wife who had shapelessly put on weight over the years, whose hair had lost its shine from wearing a headscarf, whose hands were rough from housework.

How had he and his brother ended up with such different wives?

During that one month Fehmi took it upon himself to show her and the kids around Istanbul. And, even though Mary Heather enjoyed the drive along the Bosphorus and the ferry ride to the Princes' Islands, and was even impressed by the vast dome of the 6th century Haghia Sophia and the flamboyance of the Grand Bazaar, nearly acquiring a taste for sightseeing, by the time Rafet was back, she was impatient to return to the States. However, as he chose to be with Fehmi for the main part of the day, she rarely had the chance to speak to him. The initial few times she inquired about booking their flights to America, 'There are still things I need to deal with. Just wait,' he replied.

He hadn't yet told her anything about his discussions with Fehmi.

Then one night in bed when she was pestering him for an exact date, pointing out that the children's school would be starting soon, Rafet Aslan realised that he could no longer postpone the conversation he had been dreading.

He turned on his back and, briefly glancing at her before focusing on a point on the wall, he began to explain.

He first reminded her of his predicament at work; that his job was not secure any more. Experienced employees like himself were being made redundant. Next, he said that, as she knew, they had travelled to Turkey in order to receive the inheritance; and he outlined what the situation was.

Their father had left each brother an apartment in the Galata area. There was no point in selling them; they were a good source of rental income. There was also their mother's one, as she had moved in with Fehmi and his family since their father's death. Though, for the time being, Fehmi wasn't willing to touch that place. ('The old lady keeps some of her things there,' he had said.) And he was fine with that.

The main dilemma was what to do with the business, which Kemal Bey had evenly split between his sons.

In the last couple of years the store had run down, so it was unlikely that they would be able to sell it for a decent price. And his brother had put forward an interesting proposal. He wanted to restore it and diversify the range of clothing. The country had developed significantly since Rafet had last lived here in the seventies. It was wealthier and more liberal. One effect of the liberal policies was that religion – which had until recently been suppressed – was on the rise. And currently a bourgeoisie religious class was emerging. This class was a far cry from the bearded fundamentalists with whom religion was generally associated. They loved to flaunt their wealth, wear Italian suits, drive to the Friday prayers in their sparkling Mercedes cars.

There were still hardly any shops that specialised in women's religious garments and those that did were mostly geared towards the lower end of the market. His brother's idea was to target this new bourgeoisie class. It was a good plan but he couldn't afford to do the refurbishment on his own. So he had made him an offer. It was sensible for them to be part of it. They had to think about the future of their children, about making real money.

Initially, though, the business would require a lot of work which meant that he would have to be present in Istanbul. 'And I have been trying to figure out what the best way of doing this would be. It might be that we have to move here for a period of time.'

'Rafet, just one second! Are you telling me we aren't going back?' Mary Heather asked as she propped herself up on her elbow.

'Nothing has been decided. All I am saying is that there is this opportunity. We can have our own business here. We have to consider it.'

'But Rafet, all our life is in the States. The children's school, the house, the cars, everything! How can we move here?'

'Those are all things that can be dealt with if necessary.'

At this, Mary Heather jumped out of the bed.

'We came here on holiday, so you could sort out the inheritance with your brother. And now you are informing me that we are relocating here!'

'No, I'm not. I'm saying reflect on it for a few days and we will talk again. We have not yet settled on anything.'

In the subsequent days Rafet told her that it would be good for the children, too, to spend some time in Turkey. He had noticed that they didn't understand the culture; without the language they could not connect with his family. They could try it out for a year or two. Why not? They could always go back to America if they wished.

Staying in Fehmi's flat there was little privacy, so they couldn't talk for long in the course of the day. These were all said in passing or before they went to sleep at night. And each time Mary Heather protested.

But with days the notion took root. Its presence was lurking between them. So that when ten days later Rafet said, 'We should arrange a trip to America to bring our belongings,' Mary Heather was not shocked. It sounded normal, as though they had mutually agreed.

Mary Heather had married Rafet right after university, and ever since she had depended on him. She knew no other way of surviving. Living alone with the children in Pittsburgh was something she could not even contemplate.

Another ten days later Mary Heather and their fourteen-year-old daughter Leyla flew back to America to sell the cars, put the house on the market, and have their possessions shipped. They would be trying it out in Turkey for a year.

In the days before the flight, Mary Heather was overwhelmed by the unexpectedness of what they were about to do. She could not function properly. But one strange moment stuck out.

Rafet had insisted that their son, nine-year old Ali, remain behind with him. On the plane, 32,000 feet above Europe, it dawned on Mary Heather that it was as if he didn't trust her to come back. 'He likes it here. He doesn't want to go back,' Rafet had said and Ali had confirmed, adding that Turkey was paradise, the best place on Earth.

Paradise. Best place. This was not the first time Mary Heather had heard such expressions from her son. She wondered: had Rafet conceived the idea of moving to Turkey some time ago, while they were in America? And had he been brainwashing the kids? ... Her mind flashing back to the afternoon she had returned from a week's long visit to her ailing mother in Florida... being greeted at the door by the children who kept on joyfully talking about Turkey, the sea, the warm weather... Paradise. Best place.

At the time, Mary Heather had not suspected anything; on the contrary, she had joined in, sharing their excitement for the upcoming trip to Turkey. But, now, she could not prevent tears from rolling down her cheeks. She reached for Leyla's hand – who was indifferently gazing at the sea of clouds.

Her whole life was about to change and she could not even guess what it would be like to reside in another country. Even though she had married a foreigner, she had never really been exposed to another culture. She viewed the USA as the ideal place on the planet where everyone dreamed to live but only the fortunate ones could. And she was going to leave that place to become a foreigner somewhere so far away, in a country she knew so little about.

5

Switching Skirts

In the weeks that followed, the brothers dedicated themselves to renovating the clothing store. The store was on a street that had been regenerated in the past year. The pavements had been widened and re-built with bricks; wooden benches and trees in large pots had been installed at regular intervals. Small shops were gradually being replaced by shiny emporiums. Upmarket carpet businesses aimed at tourists, modern restaurants with an Ottoman theme, spacious but minimalist jewellers lined both sides. Once dilapidated, this place could now easily be taken for a street in a Western European city.

The brothers disposed of all the previous stock by selling it in bulk. The interior of the store was re-decorated with bright cream tiles and hidden spotlights, overall providing it with an opulent feel. They changed the name of it to *Renaissance Textile Company* (spelt in English). They selected this name because it reflected what they were hoping to do – revive religious outfits, adapt them to the modern world – and, more importantly, because they wished to break with the convention of giving an establishment of a religious nature an old Turkish name. To emphasize that this was a novel movement, distinct from the past and bearded fundamentalists. That theirs was a softer version of religion that nobody should be scared of.

As for spelling it in English, that was not Rafet's idea; it was Fehmi's. It sounded even more progressive, he claimed.

At RTC staff were obliged to dress in a smart and conservative way. Although the previous staff were retained, the two new sales assistants hired wore headscarves. The store was at all times kept spotless; stock was never left lying around as in the previous days. The display windows were frequently re-designed and it was always ensured that the 90-60-90 mannequins were not revealing too much and had their heads covered.

Whereas the previous business appealed to a lower middle-class clientele, Renaissance attracted a conspicuously more affluent class. Particularly women in their twenties and thirties who looked well-groomed in their boldly-coloured headscarves and tight-fitting clothes were drawn to the store.

But also the headscarves in the windows caused them to lose out on the staunchly secular customers. As they passed by the entrance in their grey skirt suits, they muttered disapproving comments; shared with each other their worries about what was happening to Turkey; argued that secularism was under threat; and each time took a peek inside to determine what kind of people were in there, to get a view of this foreign world – this world reminiscent of Arab countries – that was slowly creeping into their republic.

**

Meanwhile, Rafet and his family moved into the two-bedroom flat that they inherited. Ali was registered at a primary school in the area. Since his knowledge of Turkish was limited he was put in year one with children two years his junior. The plan was that he would be fast-tracked by doing a semester each in year one and two.

As for Leyla, she enrolled at the same school as her cousin Seher. The Maths and Science classes were in English but all the other subjects were in Turkish, and at her age it was even more challenging to follow lectures than it was for her brother. It was out of the question for her to start from the bottom, so Rafet had suggested that she regard this as a gap year and concentrate on learning the language.

In Mary Heather's opinion it was totally ridiculous. As if they were living in a state of emergency. As if they had run away from something and had to make do. She would tell herself that she had no option but to agree to move to Turkey, for her children's sake, so the family wasn't split up.

In those initial few weeks she was plunged into loneliness. Settling in a foreign country was like trying to walk in the dark; she didn't know where the shops were, how to manage without the language, how to meet people. She felt trapped in the apartment. Days were drawn out with little to do. Fehmi found her a job at a private language school so that she could at least go out 2-3 mornings a week. Other than that, the weekly dinners they had at Fehmi's were her only social activity.

Mary Heather could imagine week after week repeating this dull cycle. For however many weeks they would be staying in this place. Until they returned to America, to Pittsburgh, to the city that was home.

She had no clue yet about the things that would break that routine. No clue yet about the role she would be playing.

In those days she was merely an observer.

The first thing out of the ordinary came at a dinner one autumn day where they saw Fehmi's older daughter Merve – who had just turned 18 – wearing a headscarf.

Merve in her headscarf and makeup was overdressed compared to everyone else that evening. She volunteered to serve the food and bring the pots from the kitchen; she was doing more than she normally would. She was so serious and was avoiding eye contact. Overnight she had transformed into another person – it was theatrical. Yet, no explanation was offered.

Up to then, to Mary Heather, Merve had seemed similar to her sister Seher – slightly older, slightly more mature, but still a teenager.

The way Merve had covered her head was different from how her mother had. As usual Tülin's flowery scarf was loosely wrapped around her head and she did not mind that some of her hair was showing. Merve, on the other hand, had her smart navy blue scarf tightly tied and had worn a white bandana underneath it to prevent any hair from accidentally becoming visible.

Throughout the dinner Mary Heather was desperate to ask Rafet what was going on, what the reason for it was, but it wasn't until they left that she could.

Rafet was strikingly casual as he shrugged off the significance of it. It was obvious that if she had not mentioned it, he wouldn't have.

'But why has she suddenly begun wearing one?' Mary Heather insisted.

'Probably she just wants to. Maybe it's because she has started university. Up till the end of high school, students have to wear uniforms in Turkey. So it is at university that they can create a style for themselves. That is when they try out new things. Some boys grow long hair. Some girls experiment with makeup. And she has chosen to put on a headscarf.'

'She looked so uneasy though... Do you think her father has forced her?'

Mary Heather was not stating what she believed had happened. She was mystified and was genuinely seeking to understand the matter.

So far, on the surface, Fehmi had been open and friendly. As Rafet had not lived in Istanbul for almost twenty years, the city and its workings were foreign to him. Hence, Fehmi helped them settle in their flat whose problems never ceased, having been occupied by elderly tenants since the '80s. He brought workmen to carry out repairs. He arranged for a private water tank to be installed which would serve them during cuts she was incapable of coping with. He drove her out to the shopping malls. He accompanied her to the children's schools for the registration. He found her a job. It was through her job that she met Barbara who would be her one and only friend in this city.

(Fehmi did all these without expecting anything in return. There was nothing unusual in this. It was the standard hospitality shown to a foreigner – to a western foreigner. To help them, to make them feel welcome and comfortable. All done with the purest of sentiments.)

But also recently Mary Heather had learned how strict Fehmi was with his daughters; that he did not allow them to go out wearing certain clothes; that he made Seher put on a long skirt to go to school.

'No, no, no,' Rafet replied wearily. 'I don't think anyone has forced her. Look at her mother: she is not covered in the same way. It's Merve's own choice, I'm sure. No one in our family wore a headscarf in the past. You see my own mother.'

Later that night when they were in bed trying to sleep, 'Did it annoy you?' Mary Heather asked.

'What?'

'That I asked about Merve.'

'No. Why should it?' Rafet snapped.

'Will Seher wear one as well when she grows up?'

'How can I know? It's a personal choice. Don't make a big deal of it.'

Although she had never witnessed him practice religion,

Mary Heather was aware that Rafet technically was Muslim. Somewhere, somewhere at the back of her mind, she had this picture of Muslim countries where women were subjugated, coerced into wearing the veil.

Would Rafet do such a thing to her?

It was already strange enough that he was a partner in a business selling headscarves. She had quizzed him about this once. 'That's business. It's not ideology,' he had said.

Despite his dismissive remarks in both of these cases, he was clearly being evasive. Why was he behaving like this? What might he be *scheming*? ... After all, just like that the Rafet she had known for so many years had relinquished their nice house with a garden and easy life with two cars in America and had relocated them to Turkey. There were no signs beforehand, no warning, merely one late night conversation, she could not have foreseen it.

What was going to come next?

When neighbours caught sight of Merve in a tightly-wrapped headscarf they raised their eyebrows. This one was not like the tulle scarf she used to wear in her early teens on the days she trotted off to the Koran course, jumping up and down with a group of her friends. The urchins playing football in the street paused to scan her.

'Everyone is free to do as they wish,' Fehmi was heard saying.

But neighbours, especially those who were not well acquainted with him, were unconvinced that he had not had a hand in this. Some feared for Merve: she had taken the wrong path; she had accepted being the second sex. When they greeted her, there was sorrow in their eyes. Men were careful not to accidentally touch her.

At the neighbourhood coffeehouse by the 14th century Galata Tower, the more secular men debated The Rise of Political Islam, citing Merve as an example of a girl who had covered up lately. They whispered that she might have joined a cult. It was a gradual movement, they argued. Bit by bit the society was becoming more conservative.

'I knew her father Fehmi when he was at university,' one old man recalled. 'He was a leftist, his hair was this long, he wore bell-bottoms this wide, with sideburns and all… And look at the man now! And his father, remember him? … Kemal Bey… He always voted for Atatürk's party. Always wore a suit. Once when the religious won the elections he hung red bikinis in the window of his shop. See how it is shifting from one generation to the next. Before we know it, they will overthrow the regime.'

'You think so?' a young man playing backgammon doubted.

'Look at what happened in Iran right next door – the Islamic revolution in 1979. They don't make an announcement before a coup. They make it afterwards.'

**

About three weeks after that dinner Leyla went to her mother Mary Heather with a curious request concerning

Seher.

Could Seher, she asked, come to their home to switch skirts in the mornings?

Being at the same school, the two girls had taken to meeting every morning to walk down the hill together to catch the bus at Karaköy. Their flat was on the way down, so Seher would first go there. As she was waiting for Leyla downstairs, now that she was safely out of sight of her parents, and now that her sister had graduated and started university, she would roll up her long grey skirt at the waist and roll down her white socks. It was her attempt to normalise her appearance, to fit in with the girls at school.

Her skirt still looked absurd as it was too wide and that was why Leyla proposed that she have a new skirt tailored and keep it at their flat.

When she asked Mary Heather for permission, 'I promise her parents won't find out about this, we won't tell anyone,' she assured her.

It was not a request for which Mary Heather had a quick, straightforward answer; not a request which she could grant without having any qualms. But also she could not ignore it. In her book, ignoring it would be tantamount to turning a blind eye to something she did not approve of; effectively, it would be no different from consenting to something which in her view was wrong.

So she agreed.

'But I don't know anything about this,' she said. She was doing a favour; being privy to their secret.

That was how Seher began stopping by their flat to switch skirts every weekday. In the morning she took off her long one and put on the short one. And after school, before going back home, she slipped into the long skirt. At the weekend Mary Heather washed and ironed the skirt along with their laundry. That way, Seher's parents remained oblivious to what was going on.

It was remarkable how much that one alteration in her look boosted Seher's confidence. She no longer held herself back when talking to her friends. She was livelier and was seen more often in the school playground.

In the coming weeks she stowed a few more items of clothing in Leyla's bedroom. Though she was exempt from Physical Education classes because of the fake sick note her father had obtained, she now participated in these and wore shorts and skimpy navy blue tights like all the other girls. On the days she met up with friends, she first went to Leyla's and put on a skirt and top that were to her liking.

In the space of a month Seher evolved so much that no one in her class was surprised when one day she was spotted with a boy. There would not be too much intimacy on school grounds. But if a boy and a girl were sitting together separate from everyone during breaks, one could assume that there was something more to it, that they were dating.

In Seher's case the relationship had developed rapidly. One evening at home she found a flower between the pages of one of her books. The colour of the flower took her back to the afternoon they were discussing their favourite colours.

46

'Blue,' he had said. 'Because it reminds me of the Bosphorus.'

She observed the boy for a full week after that, hoping for him to approach her.

Finally, on an afternoon when clubs were supposed to convene, on his suggestion they left school and went to Ortaköy. They sat on one of the benches by the Bosphorus, next to the 19th century Mecidiye Mosque that had been constructed by the Armenian imperial architects. Watching the seagulls and the hazy Anatolian side, he held her hand. Another month later, sitting on the same bench, he tried to kiss her. 'Not here,' Seher said, gently pushing him away.

They kissed at the nearby Yıldız Park for the first time. He had not planned it in advance. They were strolling in the park as usual when Seher wanted to sit under a tree. Being a weekday, there were not many people around. He sat with his back to the tree, putting his arm around her shoulder. He played with her brown wavy hair; with his finger he traced her eyelids, dimples, nose, lips... Then he shifted and sat her up, so that they were facing each other. And their lips touched. It was hardly a brush of their lips.

'I don't know,' Seher mumbled, snuggling into his chest.

A little later she lifted her head up again. Their lips touched once more. For a little longer this time.

That day, as they strode down the hill, they forgot about the other people around. Every couple of meters they paused to kiss, each time a little longer, each time a little more deeply.

6

At the Fashion Show

Towards the end of autumn the brothers organised a street fashion show at Renaissance Textile Company. In those years such events were becoming common around the country and Fehmi decided it would be a good way of advertising their venture. They hired three Russian, one Ukrainian and two Turkish models from an agency. And on the day a portable catwalk starting inside the store and extending onto the wide pavement was erected. The long-legged girls, who normally presented swimsuits and lingerie, were for the first time in their lives wearing headscarves. Although some were close-fitting, the blouses were invariably long-sleeved; the skirts were below knee length.

In terms of collection there was not the variety one would anticipate from a fashion event but still the platform was surrounded by couture enthusiasts who had been passing by. They were vying for the best positions to see the finer details of the costumes; some of them were pushing and shoving. There were even people on the balconies of the buildings around and it was not twenty minutes before the traffic was blocked.

Fehmi Aslan was caught gazing at the Ukrainian model when Mary Heather entered RTC. As that ginger-haired woman with sultry green eyes was delicately adjusting her cream headscarf, he was musing that, despite its intended purpose, a headscarf could actually be sexy – just as legs in a skirt are sexier than bare legs. He had not regarded it as such an item before. It is an interesting idea, he hummed to himself.

It was Fehmi who had invited Mary Heather, suggesting it would be a nice experience for her. There was a round table which had been brought into the shop from the office at the back for this occasion. That is where they sat, watching the event from the backstage.

Mary Heather found it fascinating that the foreign models were putting on headscarves. She also noted the contrast between the figure-hugging clothes and headscarves. Indicating this, 'What does this mean?' she asked. 'Does it mean that women who dress in this way are more moderate?'

Fehmi liked the simplicity of her reasoning.

'Yes, exactly,' he replied. 'They are more moderate. The headscarf is only a symbol for them, like the cross is for Christians.'

It was really so plain. There was nothing behind it; nothing political about it. He never understood why some people in Turkey (such as those old men in the Galata coffeehouse) complicated the matter of headscarf so much. Mary Heather with the advantage of being a stranger, in a sense with an insight akin to that of a child, had analysed it correctly.

When Mary Heather had arrived, Fehmi immediately

had spotted that she had black flip-flops on, and now, as she was surveying the store, he leaned over to call for more tea and was able to glance at her feet, which he had first beheld at the Atatürk Airport in the summer.

Later that day, Mary Heather was telling Fehmi that she had to learn Turkish. The kids, particularly the older one, were struggling at school without a grasp of the language. They had picked up some during the summer from their cousins and on the streets whilst they were playing with the neighbourhood children, but following lectures and writing were whole new dimensions. To help them improve, Rafet was insisting that they start speaking Turkish at home. Just like that, at once.

'But I can't speak it. How can we?' Mary Heather had complained.

'Then learn it,' Rafet had said.

'You can practice with us. Without attempting, you will never learn,' Fehmi remarked presently.

With her long straight blonde hair and healthy white skin, in spite of all the 90-60-90 Russian, Ukrainian, Turkish mannequins, Mary Heather had brightened up the place. She sat there so comfortably, taking up as much space as she desired, as if she were the patroness. It was impossible for anyone not to notice her presence. Yet, beneath that casualness was a woman who had only recently travelled out of America for the first time in her life, a woman who was riddled with insecurity.

Fehmi was happy, flattered even, to be sitting next to her. He was teaching her Turkish expressions when at one point, as Mary Heather was crossing her legs, his hand brushed against her thigh.

It was genuinely an accident.

Their eyes met for a split second. Because he was so stunned, Fehmi couldn't even apologise. He was ashamed that she might think it was on purpose. But something in her eyes told him she was not offended. She seemed confused. She was trying to read into this, trying to determine whether it was a signal or not.

Fehmi quickly scanned the store and established that Rafet was at the far end talking to the agency manager. He had not seen anything.

Shifting in his chair, Fehmi Aslan continued, asking Mary Heather to repeat after him. 'The Turkish flag is red and white.' But his effort to conceal his uncertainty made him serious. He couldn't regain his inspiration for interesting phrases; so, instead, he taught her the Turkish for the objects on the table – spoon, cup, plate.

When Mary Heather was leaving that day, 'You can come for tea whenever you wish,' he said. 'In the afternoons mostly we are in the office with not much to do.'

The lightness of the fashion show and the easygoingness of the foreign models to some extent eased Mary Heather's anxiety about Merve's headscarf. Since that evening she had been meticulously observing Rafet, searching for signs of change. Signs that might tell her what was going through his mind.

There was little variation in his routine compared to how it had been in America. As usual his time was split between work and home. At home, as there was no garden to tend to any more, he went into the kitchen more often, to cook what he claimed was Turkish food. Also, initially, he had taken their son to football matches, but he himself was not interested in these and after a couple of games they had stopped going.

As for his attitude towards her, perhaps he was more distant, though that could be attributed to the stress of settling in this country. In any case, they had no specific arguments to speak of yet. There were no signs of what he was plotting…

At the end of the show that day, long after the last model had gone in, some of the spectators lingered around, chatting and smoking cigarettes. It seemed like they were evaluating the afternoon. Maybe they craved for more. Or maybe they could guess that there was more to celebrate: for the girls eventually emerged from the main door to leave the venue. And their outfits this time were in stark contrast to what they were dressed in before. Some were in miniskirts, some had generous décolleté tops on.

As they cheerfully sashayed over to their Hondas or waved down taxis, the couture enthusiasts examined them and, nudging one another, whispered: 'Did you see? Did you see? That one, the one on the left, hasn't worn a bra underneath!'

**

The coverage the Islamic fashion show received exceeded even Fehmi's predictions. The event appeared in at least two newspapers. 'Sexy models have covered up,' read one, using a close-up of a Russian mannequin. 'Feast for the eyes in Istanbul,' said the second one, with a picture of the podium surrounded by the onlookers.

But the main publicity was achieved about ten days later when Renaissance was mentioned on a national television channel. It was all thanks to a Turkish model who, shortly after taking part in the RTC event, had worn a black transparent gown at another show. The incident had caught the attention of an ambitious junior reporter and the young lady was invited to a late night news programme.

That night, before interviewing her, the fat presenter indicated for the footage from the two days to be displayed side by side on the large screen in the studio. In the one on the left she was sauntering indifferently in the nightgown through which her apple-shaped breasts were clearly visible, and in the one on the right she was as grave as at a funeral as she strode wearing a Renaissance headscarf.

A grin formed on the presenter's face when he turned to the brunette model, asking for her view on the contradiction.

Not only did the model not return his smile but she adopted a frighteningly serious expression. 'Look, Mazhar Bey,' she began as stoically as she could and explained that just like she presented trousers, skirts and t-shirts, she demonstrated headscarves and swimsuits too. It made no difference whatsoever to her. 'I am a professional,' she pointed out. Then, in a melodramatic voice that did not fit in with her flawless skin, she added: 'This is my job. This is how I earn my bread.' Pleased with her performance, she tossed her hair and sat back.

'But were you not afraid of criticisms from the public for promoting headscarves?' the fat presenter pressed on. 'Some people are saying that, in a way, you endorsed that sort of clothing for ladies. What's your opinion on this?'

At this, the brunette model became furious.

'Look, Mazhar Bey,' she said sharply. 'I envy those women who wear headscarves. I wish sometimes I could cover my head too. I wish I could be the woman of my house. Public think we have a glamorous life. But do you know what? I hate the hypocrisy of this show world. I yearn for a simple life. Sometimes after fashion events do you know what I do? I lock myself into the toilet and cry!'

Part 3

Mehmet Agop

7

On a Saturday Afternoon

It was the following spring, about four months later, on a Saturday afternoon, that Mary Heather turned up at RTC. She felt like a fool the moment she entered the office where Fehmi was sitting alone, reading that day's *Milliyet*. She had been to Renaissance twice after the fashion show but both times she was with Rafet.

Fehmi was surprised, though as usual he was welcoming. It was good to break the monotony of the day. As there was not much work to do on Saturdays, generally only one of the brothers came in.

Mary Heather had been driving for more than two hours, so she was tired and sprawled on the crimson sofa. She was sweaty and her face was red. Fehmi called for tea to be brought.

'Hot tea is the best drink in the heat. You will see,' he remarked.

Then he asked how she was, inquired whether everything at home was fine, and even queried whether the taps that had recently been fixed were working properly.

On the one hand, Mary Heather needed to share

everything; on the other hand, she was desperate to forget about domestic matters, to have a respite. She was jumping from topic to topic, mostly anecdotes from the past, from America, commonplace stories, which Fehmi was attentively listening to. It was when she was talking about her mother in Florida that for no apparent reason her eyes became teary. Before Fehmi could even respond, she was crying. From Fehmi's point of view it was a queer Americanness he didn't quite apprehend.

It was unnatural for him to make physical contact or even express sympathy; however, there was no other option in such a situation. Awkwardly he sat next to her and held her hand.

'It's ok,' Mary Heather said. 'It's ok. It's nothing. Just being hysterical.'

Even when Fehmi tried to find out the cause, probing whether there was a problem at work or at home, Mary Heather didn't offer any clarification.

A little later, Mary Heather wiped her tears with a napkin Fehmi gave; then she sat back and took his hand again. There was a titillating afternoon breeze in the room now. As they sat in silence, gradually Mary Heather loosened. In that time frame, holding on to Fehmi's hand switched from consolation to something warmer.

Fehmi perceived this too and his heartbeat quickened. It would have been terrible if somebody opened the door and caught them in this position. The staff must have already deemed it odd that he was alone in the office with his brother's wife; or perhaps because she was a foreigner they had more tolerance.

They didn't move for what seemed to be a long time. Anything could have happened that afternoon but Fehmi was uncertain what the next gesture should be.

Then Mary Heather gently removed her hand from his, sat forward and drank her tea. 'I'm sorry,' she said. 'I should go.' And, just as abruptly as she had walked in, she stood up and left.

(Years later, in suburban Pittsburgh, describing this day to a friend in her kitchen overlooking the square lawn, 'It was sweet of him to hold my hand,' Mary Heather would say.)

After she departed, Fehmi had the urge to run after her and bring her back or go for a stroll together. He was struggling to decipher the meaning of her visit. Was this the opportunity? Had he missed the signal?

He wasn't sure.

This was exactly how he used to feel in his youth, with Jale at university. He couldn't read signals. It always occurred to him later, after it was too late. The significant difference of this case was that he was not a young man any more but a 41-year old father of two and the woman in question was his brother's wife.

He remembered how his hand had brushed against Mary Heather's leg at the fashion show and the expression in her eyes. Once again he went over the way she arrived today, what they talked about. And he chuckled at himself for asking about the taps.

He sat idle for a while, not thinking about anything in particular. But it was a deceptive calmness, like the silence that precedes an earthquake, for it was not long before the energy he was so familiar with was surging through him. The energy that gave him the recklessness, the courage which even astonished him sometimes. That transformed him into another person. That made him do things he could not believe afterwards.

He dialled the number. Her mobile phone.

8

At the Disused Flat

When Fehmi called, Mary Heather was still driving around in her white Renault. She wasn't yet ready to go back home. She didn't wish to be anywhere near Rafet.

After leaving RTC, she had initially driven towards the centre of Fatih and then had randomly taken roads downhill hoping to arrive at the Golden Horn. At one point she had entered a street where out of ten women eight were in head-to-toe black veils. It was a surreal sight; Mary Heather had seen the odd lady in one of those 'tents' in other parts of Istanbul but never so many of them at once. Hidden here and there she had spotted numerous churches in the Fener-Balat area. Going up a steep narrow street, she had been dwarfed by the imposing red brick façade of the Rum High School. Then, passing the Greek Orthodox Patriarchate, she had eventually managed to come out on to the road along the Golden Horn.

And she was driving by the 19th century Bulgarian Church – which quite incredibly had been prefabricated of cast iron in Vienna, shipped and assembled in its current location – thinking how cluttered with buildings

Istanbul was and that she needed some open space, some air to breathe, a wide avenue to speed on when her phone rang.

Noticing the caller was Fehmi, immediately she pulled over to the side of the road.

'Yes,' she said.

Without intending to, she sounded harsh.

Fehmi at the other end didn't even detect this. He was in full flow, ready to risk it.

'I don't know if I should be doing this...' he said, repeating the sentence he had rehearsed. 'Could I meet you some time?'

'Where?'

Her voice this time had an urgency to it that excited Fehmi.

For once he was right about his intuition.

They met at his mother's disused top-floor flat that afternoon.

Closing the door, they kissed. Then he moved her against the wall, pushed her skirt up, and pulled her top off. Dexterously, with one hand, she unfastened his belt and tugged at his grey formal trousers. She wanted more of him; she drew him towards her breasts. She didn't refrain from making noises. She was visibly relaxing, stress was leaving her body.

It was amazing how rapidly it unfolded. Yet, that was the only way possible; any talk, any words would have only stalled what was supposed to happen.

Fehmi lost himself in her large white breasts. Kissing them, rubbing his face against their softness... True, they had sagged a little but they were blooming with middle age voluptuousness.

This woman whom he had seen in casual clothes and flip-flops at the airport for the first time... this woman whose red-painted toenails never left his daydreams... this woman whom he had eyed many evenings at the dinner table... this woman who was his brother's wife... maybe that was her main quality: that she was his brother's wife.

With his each and every movement Fehmi was recalling these details. Never had lust swelled in him so much. He couldn't care less if neighbours heard them. Nothing mattered at that instant.

**

They lay on the bed side by side, smoking cigarettes, exhausted after an hour. They both were quiet. The warm breeze blowing through the curtains made them even drowsier.

Two days later Fehmi would return to this place and smell the sheets that were on the bed that day. It was at such times that the defining moment of his life recurred to him.

It had all started with going up the stairs to the Russians at the flat with drawn curtains some years ago. That was when he had learned to take risks. That was where Fehmi Aslan drew courage from. Then one thing had followed the other. Each accomplishment had led to yet another challenge, another risk, to greater ambitions. Sleeping with Mary Heather, his brother's wife, was one of the many landmarks in this secret world he had created. It was merely another step. He was experienced now and nothing frightened him.

But then sometimes he mused that the starting point was not the decision to go up the stairs to the Russians. All his deeds were linked from the very beginning. From going to university in Ankara in order to live away from home to meeting Jale, to praying for the first time at his friends' funeral, to leaving Ankara the day after espying Jale kissing the boy he resembled, to watching the river, to spending weeks contemplating in the Rüstem Paşa Mosque, to marrying the simple girl Tülin, to taking up drinking again after running into Hakan Yavuz near RTC one day, to purchasing the Soviet binoculars, to the whimsical but ultimately failed Mediterranean holiday with his wife, to discovering the Russians in high heels, the houris on earth…

Then it seemed to him that perhaps there was no other viable route; that perhaps this was how it was always meant to be. That he was mistaken. There was something called destiny.

And this was Fehmi Aslan's destiny.

**

By the time Fehmi went into the bathroom, the ashtray on the bedside table was full to the brim but there was one last cigarette in the Camel packet.

As she was smoking that cigarette, Mary Heather tried to put into perspective what had transpired in this flat a short while ago. She had grown over this past year. She had become stronger. A year ago, even a couple of months ago, she couldn't have done what she had done today. She almost couldn't believe it. She knew she didn't want to be like her friend Barbara who had got so used to her husband's vagaries she couldn't extricate herself, who had resigned to enduring life rather than living it.

How long more was life going to continue as it was? How long more would she be at the whim of Rafet? Would she feel differently after today?

Brooding over these questions, her eyes settled on the framed photograph of her mother-in-law and Kemal Bey hanging on the wall above the chest of drawers. She stubbed out her Camel and rose to examine it.

It must have been taken when they were in their 30s. Her thick black shoulder-length hair was parted on the right and she was wearing a flowery blouse with the top two buttons undone. She had the appearance of a provincial housewife dressed up for the occasion. Her serious expression, through her brown eyes, revealed an uncertainty. Kemal Bey was in his customary suit and tie, and he was striving to come across as an exemplary republican with his modern wife.

This black and white photograph was a far cry from how Fehmi's family's colour picture would be today. Tülin and Merve in headscarves, Seher in a bulky skirt… It reminded Mary Heather of Rafet's words: *No one in our family wore a headscarf in the past*, he had stressed.

On the chest were two porcelain Mevlana dancers which Mary Heather inspected with curiosity. The dustiness of the room gave her the desire to go through everything, to unearth what was beneath.

To acquaint herself with where exactly she was, she walked over to the window, and, through the gap between the curtain and the wall, she peeked down into the street.

It was getting dark. The road was so narrow that nobody was looking up, but they were also alarmingly close to the buildings on the other side. At the end of the block she could see Fehmi's apartment. There were so many endless days last summer in that place. In the flat below Fehmi's, someone was watering the plants that were on the windowsill. Further on was the 67-meter high Galata Tower with visitors on its balcony observing the fishermen on the bridges over the Golden Horn, the architectural complexity of the Haghia Sophia, the six minarets of the Blue Mosque, the ferries zigzagging across the Bosphorus...

Given the immorality of what she had just done, standing naked so near Fehmi's flat was scary. At the same time, Mary Heather couldn't deny her happiness – she was thrilled to have done this, to have crossed this boundary.

She shut the curtain tightly.

The wooden trunk below the window was so full it was half open, but in it were only bed sheets. Next to the wardrobe in the corner were a bunch of shoes, some men's, some women's, around ten to fifteen pairs, covered in dust.

She picked up a pair of cream women's shoes. From their heels she could tell they were from the seventies, yet they were in a good condition. Also among the pile were new blue stilettos that Grandmother must have bought recently but had never worn – anyhow, Mary Heather couldn't imagine her wearing them at her age.

Then her eyes caught something right in the corner.

It was a whip.

She was still holding this when Fehmi emerged from the bathroom.

He had a pink towel wrapped around his waist. He admired how comfortable Mary Heather was as she stood there completely naked; how unconscious she was of her nudity. Her broad shoulders and enormous breasts were glowing in the darkness. Normally he didn't appreciate untrimmed pubic hair, but in Mary Heather's case the black thickness of it formed a lovely contrast with her white skin. It also showed how ordinary, how natural she was. At that instant Fehmi realised what it was that made Mary Heather so attractive: her naturalness.

'I have been looking around the room,' she said with a cheeky smile. 'What's this for?'

At once a shade crossed Fehmi's face. As he was surveying her body he hadn't discerned it in her hand.

'Oh, that thing,' Fehmi Aslan said, recovering, 'It belonged to my father. It's from the Russian Bazaar. He was in the habit of buying whatever he stumbled upon in his last years.'

**

That evening when Fehmi arrived home he was more cautious than usual. As he was hanging his light spring jacket, he sniffed at it to ensure there was nothing giving him away. Unconvinced, he checked the other coats in the hallstand and paused at Merve's, baffled by the intensity of what he could smell.

He hung his jacket under his winter coat and shaped it to appear as if it had been casually placed. He took two steps back and was satisfied with the way it looked.

9

Temptation

Even though technically there was a ban on wearing a headscarf at all levels of educational institutions, at universities the implementation was inconsistent. Of the rectors who permitted headscarves, some claimed the regulation was unclear; some indicated that university students were above the age-of-consent and therefore having such a rule was ridiculous; others just couldn't be bothered.

The rectors who complied with the ban were of the belief that they were protecting the secularism of the state.

At Merve's university, Boğaziçi, the headscarf was not forbidden in those years. Founded by Americans in 1863, nationalised in 1971, the institution was a bastion of liberalism. There were barely a handful of girls who wore headscarves. It could be said that the university was out of touch with the rest of the country.

The main campus called the South was built on a hillside overlooking the Bosphorus. Dominated by American architecture that delightfully utilised the uneven terrain, on this campus girls could wear (and feel comfortable in) shorter skirts than they could outside. Couples could kiss as they wished. The plateau in the centre where students lazed around was arguably the most liberal green patch in the whole of Turkey. The language of education was English; most professors had obtained their post-graduate degrees from American universities; American terms such as schedule, shuttle, midterm, study (as in the study) peppered even the Turkish used on the campus. A good proportion of the students upon graduation left for Western countries, without even contributing to the Turkish economy, giving rise to 'brain drain' discussions.

The headscarf had never been an issue here.

Hence, nobody cared if a girl or two covered their heads.

It was only in the last few years, mainly in the Education Faculty, that there was a conspicuous increase in the number of girls who wore headscarves. Also recently, just outside the main entrance, squeezed into a small space, a mosque had been constructed at an absurd angle. It was an ugly concrete structure with crooked walls – the result of poor workmanship – that did not fit in with the neighbouring buildings. It was as though someone were imposing it on the students. (And the contrast it formed to the grandeur of the Ottoman mosques was simply undeniable.) Drinking alcohol on the campus, too, had been prohibited in the past year.

These developments were naturally concerning for the seculars, creating rumours about what was going to happen next. The frightening one was that a mosque would be erected on the South campus. The religious were maintaining that this was blatant scaremongering, devised to turn the students against them.

On the other hand, girls wearing headscarves complained that headscarves would be proscribed one day. The government would change, or a new rector would be appointed, or there would be a coup d'état – there were numerous theories about how this could occur.

But, so far, Merve hadn't encountered any difficulties.

It was all theories as it was on that spring day when she was sitting in the cafeteria with her friend Elif, watching the news on the television about the demonstration against the headscarf ban at the Istanbul University across the city.

Merve was explaining that if she were faced with a ban, she would never relinquish her headscarf, even if it meant that she had to quit university. She argued that putting on a scarf was an individual's choice; no one had forced her to and no one could prevent her from. For instance, her sister Seher would not cover her head and she was proud that the two of them were left free to decide.

Elif, however, had a different opinion.

'I have to get a job,' she was saying. 'To get a job I need a university degree. And so if I had to take off my headscarf for three or four years, then I would. I would come in a headscarf, remove it before going into lectures and then put it back on.'

71

If Elif didn't go to university, she would be stuck at home, waiting for a husband to 'rescue' her. There would be no other prospect for her. Her family were not as affluent as Merve's; her parents would most definitely marry her off – and it was unlikely that she would have a say in the matter. To move up on the social ladder, to be on a rung higher than her mother, to have more control over her life, she first had to finish university and then find a job. Having a job could provide her with the chance of having a well-educated husband; more democracy at home. With economic independence at least she would have an alternative.

Maybe. Maybe not. But at least it gave her hope.

Drawing on her cigarette, 'Wouldn't you protest against a ban then?' Merve asked.

'Probably I would… But not if there is any risk of being thrown out of university. As I've said, I will uncover my head for lectures if I have to. But once I graduate, I will search for a job where my headscarf won't give me a headache.'

Elif had never faced a dilemma over whether to put on a headscarf. Virtually every female in her family wore one, which was why she was. For her, more than a religious symbol it was a social requirement. She had been covering her head outside school since she was 15 and she admitted she would feel incomplete without one.

But her tone lacked vigour. It made it clear that she wasn't interested in the topic, that there was something troubling her.

'What's wrong?' Merve asked.

It was her upcoming Maths exam.

She had been sick much of the last week, hence had been unable to study. In the first place she wasn't good in this subject; she had failed it last term; her first midterm result wasn't promising either. She had no idea what she was going to do this time.

Merve tried to encourage her, reminding her that the last time she had complained about an exam she had received a grade well above average. She was always like this, she always complained. If she genuinely wasn't up to it, she could easily procure a sick note and write the exam later.

But, no, Elif insisted, this time it was different. 'Even if you wrote the exam now without studying at all, you would do better than I. I remember how good you did last term,' she moaned.

In response, Merve jokingly offered her services.

'No problem,' she said. 'I will take the exam in place of you.'

The girls giggled as they mused about how it would be… they built a hypothetical scenario together… Merve putting on makeup to resemble Elif… pulling her headscarf forward so her brow didn't appear so wide… perhaps she could borrow one of Elif's headscarves even… the two girls were now seeing the same vision… they realised they actually didn't look so dissimilar, Elif had a little more weight, she was slightly shorter… their laughter rose … scheming continued… gradually their mirth subsided… when merely a trace of a smile was remaining on their faces… when silence had descended...

'Do you think it's possible?' Elif asked.

Merve turned her head towards Elif, fixing her eyes onto hers. Like two virgins ready to embark on an adventure, they suggestively stared at each other. For seven or eight seconds, maybe longer. Then abruptly Merve stood up, taking her bag.

'Come on, let's go outside,' she said in an upbeat tone. 'The weather is gorgeous. We've stayed in for too long.'

That was how it began.

As an innocent reflection. Followed by a joke.

It is straightforward perhaps for one person to stealthily cheat when nobody is watching. But for two people to conspire there are more steps and each step takes more time. Establishing mutual trust, formulating the method, assessing the risk, plucking up courage, finally consenting... Overall, more time than in collaborating for something honest.

That afternoon the girls wandered in the shade behind the buildings, sharing observations about the weather, the trees, the other students... Then they sat on a bench at the View – so called because through trees one could scan the Anatolian side. Smoking Marlboros, the topic of conversation randomly shifted. To the boy Elif liked, to the blue jeans Merve wanted to buy, to the latest Hollywood blockbuster...

... and then the exam again. Inevitably, Elif went back to their previous topic. And Merve didn't object; she didn't resist the temptation, the titillation. They discussed, this time more contemplatively; but still hypothetically, still not seriously, they considered the technicalities.

For example: how thoroughly did invigilators check IDs? Would they be able to differentiate between the person in the photograph and the actual person? What about the other students taking the exam, would they notice? There would be about ninety to one hundred of them. Elif wasn't friendly with any of them; she had hardly spoken to one or two girls; most of them didn't even look at her. Some people didn't attend class; they only turned up for exams.

Then Elif reminded Merve that previously, on a day Merve had forgotten her ID at home, she had used hers to pass through the checkpoint at the university gates. They had just requested a friend to transfer the card to Merve who was waiting outside after she had gone in. It had worked then…

'Elif!' Merve exclaimed, lovingly pinching her arm. 'Anyway I have to go, tomorrow I'll see you.'

10

The Gift

Mary Heather was reinvigorated, lighter, relieved, following her first meeting with Fehmi. With pleasure she prepared interesting dishes in the evenings, taking her time over slicing and dicing the vegetables, trying out new spices. In the morning she didn't have to rush to be on time for work. In the classroom she shared stories and jokes with her language students. Everything ran smoothly. It was as if she had more hours in the day.

Their recent arguments gave her the licence to ignore Rafet at home. And she did so easily, without bothering to look him in the face. She energetically moved around, going about her own business. Lying next to him at night, she was amazed at herself that she had nothing on her conscience. Even when she tried to think about what the consequences might be if discovered, she was swiftly able to wave aside those concerns. She smiled at the person she saw in the bathroom mirror. With her wrinkles and slight double chin, she was happy with herself.

She had something to look forward to now.

Just a few days ago there seemed to be no light at the

end of the tunnel. The mistrust and anxiety that had arisen in her after their sudden relocation to Turkey had grown over the months. She had no idea why Rafet was behaving so secretively, nor where it would all lead to.

**

One Sunday morning, last January, Rafet woke them all up, saying they would be going for a drive. He forced them out of their warm beds, giving them clothes to put on.

There was no one out on the streets. Apart from the odd bakery, all shops were closed. The sky was overcast. Encouraged by the emptiness of the windy Bosphorus road, Rafet was driving faster than usual. He was refusing to provide details of their destination. Given the weather condition and the time of the day, Mary Heather and the children could guess that it was not going to be a family picnic. And when they turned into a dark wooded area, Mary Heather, scared by the surroundings that brought all sorts of dangers to her mind, tried once again: 'Where the hell are we going?'

'Yes, where to?' the children pressed on.

'Enough complaints. Be patient,' Rafet replied with a grin but without taking his eyes off the road.

Then the asphalt road came to an end and the Renault bumped along a muddy track before they eventually entered an outlandish construction site of tens or maybe hundreds of buildings. It was a large piece of land carved out of the forest. A brown island in a green ocean. All around were houses in various stages of development, some only had a foundation, others were missing the finishing touches, a couple even had people living in.

The car stopped in front of a three-storey building skeleton.

'It's this one,' Rafet said, pointing at it.

It didn't initially occur to Mary Heather.

'What do you mean?' she asked.

'This one is ours,' Rafet clarified.

Mary Heather looked like she had received an electric shock: 'Ours? You have already bought it?'

'Come and check it inside,' Rafet said in an upbeat tone, climbing out of the car.

'Inside? But where are the walls?'

It was three weeks before that Sunday that Rafet had casually mentioned a housing site being developed on the outskirts of the city where property was 'dirt cheap'. It was late at night. He was reading *Hürriyet* at the time and Mary Heather was marking exam papers.

'We should wait and see whether we will stay in Turkey before we buy,' Mary Heather had responded offhandedly. 'What if it doesn't work out for us here?'

'It seems like the right time to buy. The area will be a prime location. Prices are bound to rise.'

Unsuspecting, Mary Heather hadn't said anything else. She had presumed it was going to be one of those boring speculative conversations men tend to make.

And that was it. There had been no other talk on the subject until their drive to the forest that morning.

That day Rafet inspected every part of the structure that had nothing but pillars and concrete floors. He urged them to stretch their imagination as he showed them around what was to be the living room, kitchen, bathroom. Upstairs he drew notional walls between the pillars and let the children choose their own bedrooms, over which they started a quarrel, pleading with their father to move the wall an extra metre and add a balcony, if possible…

When Mary Heather nagged on about how he could have bought a house without consulting her, 'It's a good investment. It cost half of what our house in America did,' he answered.

'What if we leave Turkey, what will we do with this place?'

'We can always rent it out or sell it for a profit if we wanted to.'

'But it doesn't even have walls. Just look at this damn place,' Mary Heather cried. 'When will it be completed?'

'In not more than nine months. That is what the constructors are saying.'

'And who will take care of it if we leave?'

'My brother will,' Rafet declared and with that he turned around to go and view the basement.

Since that day, every Sunday morning Rafet was pulling them out of their beds and dragging them along to check on the progress the builders had made. One week they found a stack of red bricks in front of the skeleton, the other week sand and bags of cement. But by the third week the children had lost interest in these trips and when finally one day a wall appeared Rafet was the only one who was excited.

Also since then, all their savings were used to pay for the house, with Rafet refusing to enhance their current accommodation. Even when neighbours had been unable to pay their portion of the central heating bill and the heating had been cut off for a full week during the winter, Rafet had rejected Fehmi's suggestion that they have a private system installed in the flat (which in those years was the trend), arguing it would be a waste of their finances.

Despite their agreement that they would try it out in Turkey for a year and return to America if they were discontented, Mary Heather was realising that they were establishing roots here. First, Rafet Aslan had persuaded her to sell the house in Pittsburgh to fund the renovation of the clothing store. Then they had bought a house in Istanbul. Somewhere along the line the one year had increased to two years. 'We can't go back this summer, the business has to stabilise before we can. We have to stay for another year. We will go on holiday to the US in the summer,' Rafet had informed her. From time to time he remarked that he couldn't picture himself working at a company again, now that he had his own business.

Therefore, lately, Mary Heather had begun to doubt whether he would even keep his promise to visit America in the summer.

… And at lunch on that spring Saturday – the day she would go to RTC and startle Fehmi who was sitting in the office reading *Milliyet* – once again Mary Heather was demanding that they purchase the flight tickets before it was too late.

'That is not an urgent matter. It can wait,' Rafet replied. 'We have other payments to make before that.'

'When exactly?' Mary Heather snapped. 'When exactly can we buy the tickets? Soon you will say we can't go this summer.'

'I'm not saying we're not going. Wait and we will buy the tickets.'

'For every request it's the same excuse. You pledged a life of luxury but let alone travelling to America we don't even have the basics. Take this apartment: Water problems! Power problems! Heating problems! Toilet stinks, sink is blocked. Living like a bunch of rats in this garbage dump.'

'Why waste money on this apartment?' Rafet calmly reasoned. 'This place is just temporary. Our house is being built. You can have a garden and everything you want there.'

'Maybe in five years' time, yes… The house doesn't even have bloody walls! We had a house and two cars in America, remember? We had the life you are presently aspiring for!'

And with that Mary Heather dropped her fork, rose to her feet, searched for the car keys, found them under a pile of her teaching notes, and stormed out of the flat.

The lady leaving that lunch table was someone else. Someone who had suddenly been empowered. Even Mary Heather was astounded by her outburst. This is how it happens, she thought. This is how people go mad. Have nervous breakdowns. Do crazy things. Murder their husbands.

Only after she had driven past Ortaköy, did Mary Heather open her eyes to the outside world. There were so many people out strolling and fishing along the Bosphorus on that sunny Saturday. Little boys – probably simit-sellers or shoe-polish boys – were plunging into the water in their uniform white underwear. How carefree they were! Waiting at the traffic lights, among all the men fishing, Mary Heather caught sight of a girl in rolled-up jeans, helping a man who seemed to be her father. It looked so provincial, so idyllic – an image one might expect to encounter in a small sea-side town, yet they were in the heart of a city of more than ten million. Sitting on the benches, men were already drinking *Efes Pilsen*.

As always, observing other people, peering into their lives for a few moments, was refreshing but what really loosened Mary Heather were the bends in the road. Accelerating on the bends she re-discovered the joy of driving. It was as if this road had been specially designed for speeding.

By the time she turned back at Yeniköy, her recovery was complete and she was at last able to focus on herself. She was amazed once again at the turn her life had taken in the past year. If somebody had told her she would be residing in Istanbul a year ago, she would have laughed. Removed from her friends and the environment she had lived her whole life, she was so lonely.

Where could she go to in this city?
Who could she talk to?

She had only one friend in Istanbul. Just one friend.
Barbara, the English lady from her language school.

She, too, was married to a Turkish man. Her story
had a different twist. She had had a brief affair with him
in East London during which she had become pregnant.
Midway through her pregnancy he had left the country,
swearing he would return. When he hadn't, after the
birth, Barbara had flown to Turkey, having obtained his
address from a mutual acquaintance. She had arrived on
the doorstep of his family house in Tarsus with her baby
girl in her arms.

In those days Tarsus, St Paul's birthplace, was a non-
descript provincial town. There was nothing in the
centre to speak of except the Cleopatra Gate where
Cleopatra had been met by Marc Anthony on her trip
from Alexandria two thousand years ago. (Barbara had
giggled at the irony of this when she had mentioned it to
Mary Heather.)

It was the first time his family had come into contact
with a foreign person and they had warmly welcomed
her with the customary Anatolian hospitality. So he had
to put on a face and acquiesce to the marriage.

Here she was 15 years later, now living in Istanbul,
still married, with two teenage daughters. Somehow the
marriage was going on, albeit she had much to be
disgruntled about. She had suffered physical abuse a
number of times when the kids were younger. *He would
grab my arms and shake me, leaving me bruised.* Her

husband was unable to hold down a job, walking out each time after arguing that he should be given an engineer's responsibility, though he was merely a technician with qualifications from some obscure college in London. Practically she was the main breadwinner, yet she was barely allowed to visit her family in England – she had even missed her mother's final days five years ago, landing in London two days after her death.

In her conversations with Mary Heather on her balcony which had a delicious view of the Bosphorus, Barbara sometimes touched on divorce. It wasn't exactly economics that stopped her from getting a divorce (teaching English in Turkey she could manage on her own): she was afraid that her kids would be taken away from her. She had heard second-hand accounts that the Turkish parent was favoured in such cases, though she had not established what the law was. And anyhow she couldn't trust the law in Turkey.

Although she and Barbara were characteristically unlike each other (Barbara with her primness, insistence on having proper English breakfast tea, and excitement at Marks and Spencer opening in Istanbul), the fact that they were both foreigners married to Turks had created a common ground.

Now, cruising along the Bosphorus in her Renault, Mary Heather was reflecting on Barbara. The bitter truth was that Barbara couldn't divorce her husband because she had got accustomed to the way she was living; however uncomfortable, restrictive, nasty it was, that was her *comfort* zone. Mary Heather feared being like Barbara in 10 years' time, stuck in life, complaining but doing nothing to improve the situation.

When she reached Kabataş, she chose to drive on. She wasn't ready to go back home. Nor did she wish to see Barbara today; sitting on the balcony, drinking *Tetley* tea and commiserating, was the last thing she needed. She was tired of her company. If she had been in America, probably she would have reduced the frequency of her visits. But here what alternative did she have?

At Karaköy she crossed the bridge over the Golden Horn and steered all the way up to the Haghia Sophia. She had hardly been around this area before. The only place she knew was RTC and that was why she went there.

And there she found Fehmi Aslan sitting alone in the office at the back of Renaissance Textile Company reading *Milliyet*.

**

It was five days later that Mary Heather's phone rang again and without any hesitation she got into the car for the short drive to her mother-in-law's flat. As she was parking, it occurred to her that someone might spot the car. But the white Renault was quite indistinguishable she decided.

Mary Heather's memory of their first meeting was hazy. That day they both were full for their own reasons. Things had unfolded so rapidly that it had a dream-like quality. It was at the second rendezvous that Mary Heather was able to identify some of Fehmi's finer traits.

What intrigued her most was his enthusiasm.

There was something of a teenager in his desire, his hunger. At the same time, he was distant as if he were privately enjoying being with her, as if this were a solitary activity. For instance, now, the way he hovered over her breasts, his intensity, he seemed to be imprinting the shape of them on his mind. Or now: he had closed his eyes and was rubbing his chin, his lips, his nose, his eyelids on her large firm nipples.

Years ago, in her early twenties, though she had been shy, Mary Heather had been proud of her breasts. Sometimes she went out alone without wearing a bra underneath her t-shirt and relished the intimate moments when a boy noticed it. Even to this day, more than sex, she loved foreplay involving her breasts. To experience them being appreciated after all these years was majestic. She ruffled Fehmi's hair and, 'Come here,' she laughed, pulling him closer.

Later, lying next to her, he rested his head on her breasts as he would on a pillow, wallowing in their softness. Even though she couldn't see it, she could feel his eyes were fixed on her feet. It reminded her of that day at the fashion show, when, on the pretext of ordering tea, he had leaned over and gazed at her feet. Like that day, today her toenails were painted bright red.

Mary Heather was not mistaken: next, Fehmi sat up

and took her left foot in his hand. He first held it as one holds a sculpture, admiring it in its entirety, and then he examined its details, caressed her toes one by one, concentrating on her second toe that was a little longer than the big one.

So it didn't surprise her that, when she was dressing, Fehmi Aslan picked up her size 38DD black lace bra, sniffed at it at length and asked, 'Could I keep this?'

11

From an Ortaköy Café

Sitting in the classroom in Anderson Hall on the South Campus, Merve was ready and focused. Her hands were cold and there was a controlled calmness about her. Receiving the signal, she began to write the exam as quickly as she could. She realised something peculiar: under added pressure she was faster than usual; her thoughts were clearer; she was more succinct in her answers, more to the point.

She was already more than halfway through when the teaching assistant came to check her identification card. The underpaid assistant, dressed in beige formal trousers, white sneakers and a red & black floral sweater, was a third year PhD student who had stayed on following his undergraduate degree to avoid going out into the 'real world'. He was moderately satisfied with his research work in front of the computer but he hated the teaching duties. He was resentful that, unlike some of his friends, he hadn't been able to secure a scholarship from a North American university for his post-graduate studies.

As he was inspecting Elif's ID, he was also keeping

an eye on the class. Merve had pulled her headscarf forward to cover part of her forehead. She didn't look up at the assistant when he arrived, pretending to be engrossed in her papers.

Of the ninety-seven students in that hall she was the only one wearing a headscarf.

At the late afternoon teaching sessions, the assistant had seen this girl sitting alone; it had seemed like she had no friends in that class. His grandmother was the sole person in his circle who covered her head, and, in her case, she used a traditional tulle scarf. He had nothing against the girls in headscarves. 'I don't care,' he would say. 'If they wish to cover up, they can.' But also the headscarf was a barrier that prevented him from socialising with them; he would instinctively conclude that they wouldn't have anything in common.

Merve's heart was beating wildly now. She was wondering why the scruffy assistant was taking so long. She had not been able to write anything whilst he was standing next to her.

The assistant's little game was to nose out the birthdates of the students. He noted that this girl was a year older than the normal age for this group. And April 20th, was that Taurus or Aries? The underpaid assistant was annoyed that he couldn't recall. He verified that the name the girl had written on the exam sheet matched what was on the ID. Elif, an old-fashioned name. Then he ticked the box on his list and moved on to the next person.

The moment he left, Merve felt her limbs relaxing. Blood was once again freely flowing through her veins.

She gently wiped the sweat off her palms and tried to concentrate on the remaining questions. But with around one hundred people breathing, the room had become airless. And exactly at that point this oppressive atmosphere descended on Merve, causing her to perspire profusely.

By the time she reached the last question, the clarity in her thinking had gone. Her handwriting was barely legible. She paused for a while for her hand to rest. When she attempted again, her writing resembled a seven-year olds'.

Was her mask slipping?

She had to stop. What she had done was sufficient for a reasonable grade. It was unnecessary to risk it any longer. She was going to sit back, cool down and then hand in her papers. She scanned the hall; no one had finished yet. She had to hold out for a little more. The assistant in his distinctive sweater was now sitting at the lecturer's desk, staring out of the window. Even from that distance she could tell he had a big head. Then he sneezed and removed a grotty American flag handkerchief from his pocket and blew his nose into it. His slovenliness eased her mind.

At that instant Merve sensed that she was being watched.

Her gaze shifted towards the blonde girl standing by the blackboard. She hadn't noticed her before; she must have entered midway through the exam. She was the assistant of this subject last term when Merve was taking it. Her presence, Merve deemed, was not a good omen. She lowered her head and put her hand on her brow. The blonde girl's eyes were firmly fixed on her until finally a boy in the front put his hand up and she went over to him.

In the meantime, a few people had completed and left. This was the right time to go as she could elude the blonde assistant.

With an exaggerated composure, Merve Aslan gathered her sheets and pencils, and climbed out of her seat. After she took a step, to make it seem more natural, she turned and checked the desk as if she were ensuring she hadn't left anything behind, and then confidently strode over and submitted Elif's exam papers.

She met Elif at the Steps, the popular meeting point overlooking the green plateau.

It was a splendidly sunny day and there were so many people lazing on the grass, chatting, playing backgammon, kissing. The ever-present American football player with shaven legs was strutting in his tiny pink shorts, with two of his lackeys marching behind him. Nobody knew how many years he had been at this institution or which department he was studying at or in fact whether he was a student at all. Right in front of them the pudgy economics professor who also was a famous football pundit had just arrived in his cramped red antique car and was having trouble getting out of it. A step below them, a girl wearing a headscarf was leaning on the shoulder of her boyfriend whose hair was tied in a ponytail.

'How did it go?' Elif asked.

From having controlled herself for almost two hours,

Merve needed to release energy. She wanted to scream and run. But it was stupid to be meeting so near the building where the exam was. They couldn't afford to be seen together.

'I will tell you later. Come on, let's go down to Bebek,' she said, leading the way.

Once they were on the shady road which zigzagged down to Bebek, Merve was visibly relaxed. She was skipping down the stairs that linked the distinct levels of the road.

In their excitement, neither of the girls spotted the boy and the girl partially shielded by the bushes and trees. They were kissing eagerly, in the way young lovers do, and the boy had his hand inside the girl's white blouse. Hearing the passers-by, the girl restrained the boy and they shared a giggle, waiting for it to be clear again. Further down, a second couple, ignoring the ban on alcohol, were openly drinking *Efes Pilsen*.

There was no one at the tennis court which in places was still covered in leaves. As they turned the final corner and were heading for the Bebek Gate, the sun hit them in the face. The swimming pool hadn't yet opened for the season and, through the fence, they could see it was full of murky water.

Coming out of the gate, they crossed the road, to walk along the Bosphorus towards Bebek. Merve indicated that the *FOR RENT* sign on most of the moored yachts was in English. Elif chuckled but didn't say anything.

'Where shall we go?' Merve asked.

'How about Bebek Kahvesi?'

'You know, I'm actually quite hungry, I have to eat something. Where in Bebek can we eat?'

'Let's go to McDonald's. We can get the food and eat it at the park, sitting on a bench by the Bosphorus.'

Merve never understood Elif's love affair with McDonald's and the greasy food just didn't feel right in this weather.

'How about we go to Ortaköy instead?' she asked.

'Ortaköy would be super. Good idea!'

In less than thirty seconds the girls were in a yellow taxi speeding down the Bosphorus.

**

In Ortaköy they directly went to the stalls that sold *kumpir*, stuffed jacket potatoes, and stood by the Bosphorus, to the left of the Mecidiye Mosque, as they ate.

Afterwards they didn't discuss where to sit. The cafés in the backstreets were improving but Ortaköy meant the ones facing the main square. Food wasn't good at these establishments, which often is the case with special locations – one is charged for the location, not the quality of the food. So the girls satisfied themselves with hot drinks and cigarettes.

Only after they had comfortably settled was Merve ready to properly recount how the exam had gone. Having accomplished her mission, she was brimming with confidence. She assured Elif that the assistant hadn't noticed anything.

'He can't care less about the exam. He is weird

anyway with that big head and disgusting American flag handkerchief of his. Most of the PhD students are... I was more concerned when I saw that gorgeous blonde assistant towards the end. You know, she was the assistant last term.'

'Did she recognise you?'

'No, no, don't worry. I left shortly after anyway.'

'I won't go to class for a couple of weeks, so they totally forget my face. I hope they won't pick up anything from the handwriting.'

'Don't worry so much. Relax. The more anxious you are, the more suspicious you will appear. Let's just not talk about it.'

It had been a while since Merve had last come to Ortaköy. At high school there was a period when she spent her every Saturday afternoon here. It was here at the age of 16 that she had first smoked.

In those days she was unhappy at school – the private school she was attending with her sister Seher. As she had grown older, the differences between her and the rich secular students had become more pronounced. There were those girls who flirted with boys during breaks, those who virtually invited them to lift up their skirts or had water fights so fierce that by the end their black brassieres showed through... Those boys who came to the afternoon classes stinking of beer... She couldn't stand the way they treated the teachers who generally were from less affluent backgrounds; mocking their accents, manners, outfits... She couldn't believe how much they disregarded the

Religious Studies teacher, who was selected by the school board because he looked like he would be lenient with these rich kids; wouldn't force them to recite prayers; would turn a blind eye to cheating in exams. They would bring snacks and fizzy drinks to his class; tell the poor man they had sampled pork to test if he would be provoked...

She felt an outsider with her long skirt among those kids.

She was only friendly with one or two hard-working bespectacled girls who sat in the front rows. But they were no soul mates. Her best friends were from the neighbourhood they lived in. They were from more traditional families, their fathers were strict like hers; their mothers didn't spend their afternoons at the hairdressers having their hair dyed blonde or at parties playing cards; they weren't bothered if the cutlery at their supper table didn't match; in the evenings they sat altogether and ate heartily-prepared meals; they went to state schools; regardless of anything they respected their teachers and elders; on the bus they gave up their seats to them...

At that time Merve was also observing how religious people were evolving in Turkey.

On the one hand, she would remember herself at the Koran course in the 14th century Arab Mosque sitting on the smelly carpet in front of the Imam who rode an old *Bisan* bicycle, wore a threadbare green sweater his wife had knitted 20 years ago, and issued messages of austerity and spirituality... His was a faith imported from another space and time, a faith on the peripheries of the city life, 'The Islam of the Desert' perhaps...

On the other hand, there was the emerging bourgeoisie religious class, with smart and assertive women flaunting brand name garments and young men in Italian suits driving to the Friday prayers in their sleek Mercedes cars. A class that capered on rented yachts in the Mediterranean. 'The Islam of the City'...

Sitting at the cafés with her friends, Merve would find herself biting her nails as she brooded over these dichotomies, striving to figure out where she would fit in.

Then one day she took a cigarette from an older friend's Marlboro packet lying on the table and lit it. She hadn't premeditated this and there was no joy, no giggles. Not like teenagers playing with cigarettes as if they are bubble-makers.

But like a labourer she drew on it deeply and profoundly.

It was also here last autumn that she conceived the idea of putting on a headscarf.

Like any ordinary girl Merve aspired to dress in a tasteful way that mirrored her personality and have a like-minded boyfriend. Given the restrictions at school, it was always at university that she imagined she could define her appearance. Define how to look in life, how to present herself to the world, to the opposite sex. Headscarf was part of that. It was her indication to the society of her viewpoint.

When she broached the subject of wearing a headscarf with her parents, her father's reaction was surprising: he was taken aback.

Fehmi was well aware, of course, that Merve was more conservative, more interested in religion than her sister Seher. At school she had willingly put on a skirt that was longer than the other girls'. Whereas her younger sister each time had searched for an excuse to skip the Koran course, Merve had made it a point to memorise all the prayers. And, yes, his wife wore a headscarf; and, yes, it was him, Fehmi Aslan, who had demanded her to years ago, but so much had transpired since then. And a daughter – whom he had witnessed growing up and whom he could still recall as a little girl – wanting to cover her head was a much more delicate matter. It was a decision that could influence the rest of her life.

In reply he told her that it was her choice; if she wished, she could. 'But have you considered it carefully?' he asked. He pointed out that some universities banned it and she might experience difficulties at some stage during her education. If she were compelled to remove it or if she voluntarily chose to remove it, once she had grown used to wearing one, there would be social implications which she also had to take into account.

Merve had not anticipated such a discourse from her father. She had presumed that he would be outright happy.

Her mother's response, in contrast, was succinct.

'It's up to you,' she said. 'After this age, it's all up to you.'

In any case, Merve was adamant.

Before she went out in a headscarf, upon her father's suggestion, she agreed to try it at home for a week... And on the third day of her trial period Mary Heather saw her and wondered why she was so uneasy and whether her father had coerced her into covering up...

Now, as she lit another cigarette, Merve's mind went back to the exam. How had she found the courage? What would she have done if she had been detected? It was always afterwards that she truly weighed the gravity of her actions.

She turned her head towards the square.

She loved Ortaköy. There was a leisurely activeness here. Students, painters, pensioners, lovers, pigeons, simit sellers, shoeshine boys, the mosque with its two minarets, the jewellery market... The perpetually wavy Bosphorus which could narrate the history of Constantinople through the articles lying on its bed... The Ukrainian tankers which came threateningly close to the shore... The grey suspension bridge that an English artist was proposing to paint in the colours of the rainbow... The hills on the Anatolian side that gazed at the more attractive European side like a jealous sister...

As she was savouring this view, reflecting on her day, her courage now seeming unreal, through the smoke lingering in the air, Merve caught sight of a boy and a girl standing by the Bosphorus.

They had their backs to her; their arms were wrapped around each other's waists. The girl's head was resting on the boy's shoulder. Rising on her toes she gave him a kiss on the cheek.

They were beautiful, Merve thought. So beautiful that it would inspire a poet to pick up his pen, a musician to compose, a painter to paint.

'What are you looking at?' Elif asked, interrupting her.

'Nothing,' Merve replied. 'I'm musing.'

Then the boy and the girl turned round and strolled past the café.

Seher Aslan was too absorbed to discern her older sister watching from behind the ivy and Marlboro smoke.

12

The American Dream

Mary Heather met Rafet at a dance club in Pittsburgh, PA, when he was a third year university student.

After Fehmi had quit university, their father had resolved to put together all his savings and send Rafet to America. His mother was worried at the time of his departure and prepared food for him to take with him. 'What will you eat there?' she reasoned. Kemal Bey had a different kind of anxiety. 'Don't go there and turn into an extremist – fascist or religious,' he warned him. 'Study, learn and return to serve your country.' Although by then he had switched his interest to religion, Fehmi had retained his leftist roots and he was resentful that his brother was going to the capital of capitalism. 'Don't become assimilated,' he simply said.

As for Rafet himself, he was full of optimism. He was going to the Space on Earth. 'Don't forget us. Phone us,' the family had requested, waving goodbye at the airport. 'Tell us how life over there is.'

In America, Rafet was dazzled by how high the buildings were, how wide the roads, how large the cars, how big the people, how much more the portions at the restaurants.

Overnight he had transformed into a smaller person.

He would turn round and stare at the enormous people he came across on the street. Some were so fat it was impossible to identify their breasts, bottoms, necks; their legs and arms resembled Hoover bags. Peering up at the skyscrapers he would feel dizzy. He was caught jaywalking twice. At night the wail of ambulance sirens never seemed to cease. When going out, he was always attempting to pull the doors that had to be pushed.

Above all, though, he was astonished by the girls. They were so easy-going, physically so fit, their features so perfect. As if they had been manufactured using a magical formula.

... And so at the orientation day of the university's Turkish Student Association, within five minutes of meeting Rüstem, Rafet was talking about the blonde girls. In those initial few months, every weekend they went to dance clubs together. Rüstem was the more active one. He was from the Turkish Navy and he claimed to have a wealth of experience with females which he was fond of relating over and over, glorifying his achievements a bit more each time in the manner of a fisherman. In America he called himself Rüs.

Rüs tried hard: he danced in front of the girls, placed himself next to them on couches, asked for cigarettes. Guessing the long-haired blondes might be prejudiced against Turks, there was even a time when he introduced himself and Rafet as Italian, relying on the physical similarities of Italians and Turks.

But nothing worked.

Each and every time the Pennsylvanian girls politely slipped away.

Dejected after four months, they stopped frequenting nightclubs. Instead, Rafet focused on his studies. He was going to academically prove himself to Americans. He wasn't satisfied with having only Turkish friends, he genuinely wished to be more integrated, yet his relationship with Americans was limited to lectures and the occasional frisbee game on the campus.

During that period, Rafet grew more observant of life in America. He never turned against the USA as such, but he noted for instance how black people were still segregated from the whites. Majority of the black people dwelled in ghettos which wealthier whites didn't dare to enter; there were dingy nightclubs with exclusively black clientele; percentage of blacks at his university was significantly lower than in downtown; a disproportionate number of blacks were in menial jobs...

Whenever he stumbled upon dirty public toilets, homeless people, streets strewn with rubbish, scenes that in his view undermined America's status as The Most Developed Country in the World, he took photographs.

He also phoned his family more often – usually on nights when he had been drinking *rakı* and listening to Turkish music. He would say he was 'just about managing'. He was able to procure packaged Turkish food from a store downtown but it was nowhere near as tasty as the homemade. Sometimes his friends brought *rakı* from New York but otherwise he had to make do with the Greek ouzo. Flavourless chicken breasts, the perfunctoriness of the American barbers, the lack of Turkish films were some of the other grievances Rafet had.

At the end of such calls, he was overcome with loneliness and yearning, and fell asleep, sometimes on the couch, sometimes on the carpet by the blue telephone.

At the first opportunity Rafet flew to Turkey on holiday.

Family and neighbours alike were eager to hear his stories from America. They were amazed at how laid-back he had become, putting his feet on the table, wearing flip-flops, shabby jeans and a t-shirt with holes in it. Rafet relished the attention, revelled in being the special one, but it also made him think that he had progressed, that he was at a higher level than the people he had left behind merely a year ago.

One evening he was denied entry into a Taksim nightclub wearing his flip-flops. Taken aback, 'Where is this rule written?' he demanded to know and asked to see the manager of the establishment.

'I'm the manager,' the bouncer maintained, placing his palm on Rafet's chest.

Rafet wasn't in the mood to laugh. So he stood his ground, insisting on communicating with someone further up in the hierarchy.

Noticing the customer wasn't backing off, the second bouncer poked his head in. 'The manager is in a meeting, brother, alright?' he said and seemed quite pleased with himself for inventing this excuse, believing it had shut up the boy who was trying their patience. 'Come on, brother,' he added, indicating the way out.

Wavering between giving up and uttering the most offensive swear he could conjure up, Rafet spotted a girl inside who had a smarter pair of flip-flops on. 'What about her?'

This time the bouncer had had enough; he had no sympathy for people who spoke too much. He wrapped his heavy hand around Rafet's throat, pushing him away from his door.

In the ensuing squabble Rafet said something to the effect that he resided in America and that there nothing such as this would occur. He didn't know where to go to, who to complain to.

After that day, Rafet was easily irritated by the inefficiencies he encountered. The chaos of the traffic infuriated him. Something as elemental as returning a purchase was a hassle. In this country one always had to be alert to avoid being cheated in the most basic of transactions.

That one incident with the flip-flops had opened the floodgates, bringing back memories of all the things that annoyed him about Turkey. Life was simpler in the US; in everyday life, in matters such as these there were rules and everyone stuck to the rules.

It was then that Rafet Aslan decided he was not going to live in Turkey.

Somehow, somehow he had to manage in America.

This was the man who years later would just as lightly make his mind up to relocate to Turkey. The process was similar in the two cases. A couple of hot issues fuelled his judgement, prompting him to dismiss a country in its entirety. And in both cases he ignored the drawbacks of the place he was choosing.

For him, choosing a place actually meant dismissing another.

At that time, in 1998, he feared redundancy. And when his brother offered him an alternative, proposed that he be a partner in the business, that one concern over his job evoked everything he disliked about America. It reminded him how lonely life there was. Apart from his wife and children, he had nobody.

One evening, shortly after he had completed his military service, watching the Turkish national football team on television, he recalled how dull American sports were. In his twenty years there, he hadn't been able to apprehend the lure of American football, baseball or ice hockey; basketball was the only sport that mildly interested him. Soccer was virtually non-existent.

'Come on, lions!' he was shouting at one point, urging on the players.

'But, dad, you don't even like soccer,' Leyla remarked, interrupting him, and a grin appeared on Fehmi's face.

Later that evening, Rafet explained that no one from Mary Heather's family would help them if they had an urgent need of cash or if their car broke down or if they had a problem with their house. There was none of the support one could expect from family in Turkey.

'If you go into a house when they are eating, they will not invite you to join them. They will finish their meal, and then come and sit with you,' he complained. 'Lately I have been thinking that I don't want my children to grow up to be like that. I want them to learn Turkish culture, Turkish hospitality.'

All the while, Mary Heather was sitting there, not understanding a word of what was being said. Rafet never shared these bothers with her. The sole reason he gave for their move to Turkey was the predicament he was facing at his work.

By his third year in America, academically Rafet was successful. Socially he was resigned to not having American friends and seeking pleasure in the activities of the Turkish Student Association. They had Turkish food festivals, Turkish film shows, picnics with barbeques at the weekends, football matches… Events which were full of longing for Turkey. On special days they organised entertainment with a Turkish singer and a belly dancer from Manhattan.

As it transpired, at one of these, the 29th October Republic Day celebrations (an event they all snubbed when back in Turkey), Rafet ran into Rüstem whom he hadn't seen for a while. Rüstem at once began talking about his new girlfriend: a 45-year old schoolteacher whom he had met at a Latin dance club in the Shadyside district. She was a divorcee who was weary of American men and had gone on a Salsa course to increase her chances with foreigners. 'Do you know how old I am?'

she had asked one night when Rüstem was trying to undress her at his flat.

'But she doesn't look like she is forty-five,' Rüstem was now telling Rafet. 'And her face is not such that you can't stand looking at it...'

'Rüstem!' Rafet exclaimed. 'I've missed you. We should go out one night to remember the good old days.' So that was how, just for once, they went out again. This time to a new club in the South Side.

After his customary single Budweiser, Rüs took to the floor, making strange movements in front of the girls – lifting his knees up to his belly, turning on his heel, clapping his hands as if to another tune playing in his head. And that night he was having moderate success with one brunette laughing at him.

By then, Rafet had no intention of meeting anyone at a nightclub. He had decided that clubs were not the right site to search for a proper girl. He was keeping a low profile, standing aside, gazing at the people dancing, when he came eye to eye with Mary Heather.

She was leaning against a pillar and seemed bored, as all of her friends were dancing. She was slightly overweight but in a nice, tidy way. She had no makeup on; her clothes were what she had put on in the morning: a pair of jeans, a loose white t-shirt, flat leather sandals. She was a little uneasy, unsure of herself. She clearly was not a nightclub person. Rafet presumed she had been forcefully brought out by her friends.

That night he didn't deem her wonderful or breathtaking. He was simply trying his luck with a kind of American girl he had never before. So he was relaxed when he went over to talk to her. In his company she too relaxed. She was a year older than him, a student at his university. They discussed their courses, her five-year plan in life, how to lease a car, health insurance, that sort of stuff. At the end of the night when he asked for her phone number, she was surprised and delightfully gave it.

They met at his local pizza eatery for lunch the next day. It was a basic joint with green diner booths, squeezed between a grocery and a dollar store. The owner was an American-Italian who wore a medallion around his neck and sat on a high stool at the till collecting money and issuing orders to the staff. The pizza was decent and the casual atmosphere suited them both.

'I love that you can sprinkle extra shredded cheese on the pizza in this place,' Rafet remarked.

Mary Heather smiled at this observation.

'I had never thought of it as something special, but you're right, it makes a huge difference,' she replied.

Starting from that first date, Mary Heather was amused by Rafet's attention to small things which she overlooked; she found him cute at the times he sought the right word in English to express himself. She would have preferred an American boy – or, even better, somebody from Pennsylvania – but it didn't matter that much that he was a foreigner. She was grateful to finally have a boy who cared for her, who called her in the evenings. She didn't know anything about Turkey (she was convinced that Rafet was joking with her when he swore the language of Turkey was Turkish and not Arabic), nor was she eager to discover. She assessed Rafet without any prejudice, purely from what she obtained about him as an individual. Her mission was to have a boyfriend, and later a husband, a family, an ordinary life.

As for Rafet... He liked Mary Heather's plainness. He liked that she was not judgemental. He liked that she was penny-wise. He liked that she enjoyed sex as much as him and that she did not refrain from making noises as she came. But, more than anything, Rafet liked that she was American. That he finally had an American girlfriend!

Through her he learned about contemporary American families. Her mother was a nurse, a single parent. She had one younger sister who was severely obese and was spending all her time eating junk food in front of the television. Her father, whom she hadn't been in touch with for nine years, had re-married and had three other smaller children. No one in her family had been abroad except an uncle who had served in a military base in Japan.

They married right after graduation. Rafet was the first foreigner to enter the family, and, at gatherings, her mother was unable to stop herself from whispering comments about him. Rafet never heard these in full; he would catch words or notice something in the air, but he chose to ignore. (Only in the later years did he gradually reduce his visits to his mother-in-law, before giving up totally, providing an excuse each time, never being explicit about his disturbance.)

Despite having a degree in chemistry, Rafet couldn't find a relevant job; so he took up an administrative role at a shipping company. And she was employed as a high school teacher. In American standards, they never had much money but they were never short either. They had a mortgage on a house in the suburbs of Pittsburgh and two cars. They lived an uneventful, orderly life, and derived bliss from going to the shopping malls and having barbeques in the garden at the weekends.

Rafet was content with life in those days. As long as he obeyed the rules and laws, as long as he put up with the tedium of work, he would have a reasonably prosperous existence. Above all, he appreciated the security of it. He was not keen to holiday in Turkey ('The flight would be exhausting for the children,' he would tell his parents.). He went back only once in the '80s during his mother's illness.

Then in 1998 after his father's death they travelled altogether as a family, as he had to sort out the inheritance and do his military service which he was having trouble postponing. That was the first time his wife and children had gone to Turkey.

And, at that time, Rafet Aslan was not feeling secure in his life in America any more.

13

Sisters at Night-time

What she had seen in Ortaköy helped Merve forget any distress she had over the exam. That evening at supper she observed her little sister.

Seher had always been more inclined than her to the light pleasures of life. Merve would imagine that perhaps at university with more freedom she would gradually drift away from the family. Then when the time was right she would marry someone whom their father would not heartily approve of. Or perhaps at some point she would just give in, accept the family's way of living...

In any case, today's discovery was completely unpredictable. The boyfriend, the kiss, the truancy, the mystery of the skirt... her little sister's secrets...

She wondered, should she tell her or should she keep it to herself?

She turned to their father who was slurping his lentil soup as he was following the news. Often he seemed preoccupied with something else. Her mother, on the other hand, was at all times concerned with the present, as she was at this moment, asking whether anyone

111

wanted more soup. Grandmother as usual was sitting in her corner, disgruntled.

Later that evening, after everyone else had gone to bed, the two sisters remained alone in the living room. They were both studying and on the television was the fat presenter's late night news programme.

He had two guests with him. One was a 31-year old unemployed construction worker who three days ago had threatened to jump off the Bosphorus Bridge for the second time in the last four months; and the second one was a retired *Fenerbahçe* footballer who had been driving by in his BMW and had stopped and persuaded the man not to jump by pledging to find him a job.

'But every time you lose your job do you get the urge to throw yourself off the bridge?' the presenter was pressing.

'Not every time,' the unemployed man casually replied. And recounted that he had knocked on every door he knew for a job and had no option left. At home he had five kids and a wife to feed; he could no longer look at their faces.

The fat presenter asked some other questions, advised the man not to climb over the balustrades again, and then announced the commercial break, after which they would be debating the dilemma faced by a 25-year old hermaphrodite who was confused over whether to stand in the front with the men or at the back with the women during prayers. The person in question had been forbidden by the Imam from entering the village mosque and ostracised by the community…

'I hate this man,' Seher said, indicating the fat presenter.

'I heard the other day that he has bought himself a two-million dollar mansion by the Bosphorus with his earnings from this nonsense.'

'Only in Turkey this is possible… I'm going to switch over. Are you watching this?'

'No, no, you can go ahead.'

Seher surfed the channels and disinterestedly returned to the one showing a Turkish sex movie from the '70s.

'Which channel do you prefer?' she asked, lowering the volume.

'Doesn't matter. Let it stay here,' Merve replied.

As on the screen half-naked people in white cotton underwear were running about, frolicking, screaming in a bedroom, the sisters pretended to study. They both took furtive glances at the television, occasionally making irrelevant comments.

At times such as this the night felt quieter and colder.

Neither of the sisters would believe if somebody told them that some twenty years ago a youthful Fehmi Aslan (in love with a blonde girl who wore black miniskirts and painted her nails burgundy) would surreptitiously go to the cinemas to learn from these very same pictures – which had been unearthed thanks to the boom in the private television industry in the '90s (as they been buried by the junta of the 1980 coup d'état).

Meanwhile, their mother, rolling in bed, unable to sleep, had pricked up her ears to distinguish the noises coming from the living room. She could guess what her daughters were watching.

'He is a handsome boy,' Merve whispered from across the table.

It cut through the silence of the night. There was a twinkle in her eyes and Seher immediately thought of her boyfriend.

'Who?' she asked nevertheless.

'I saw you today. You look lovely together,' Merve said.

Merve had nothing against what she had espied from that Ortaköy café. She dreamed of a world where everyone lived as they wished provided that they tolerated one another. If her sister wanted to wear a miniskirt, she respected that. If she wanted to have a boyfriend, she was happy for her to.

She was proud of having a sister who was different from her.

Her sister's freedom to do as she willed was proof that she herself had not been coerced into putting on a headscarf, that she was covering her head of her own volition.

That night Merve stayed in the living room studying. Lately she had taken to sleeping there on one of the divans. When 15-year old Seher went into the bedroom, she took a cigarette from her sister's Marlboro packet concealed under her black lace bras and smoked by the open window.

Merve had tried to comfort her, swearing she

wouldn't say anything to their parents. Still, it troubled Seher that she had found out. After she finished smoking, she stood by the window a little longer, relishing the breeze on her face. Then she removed all her clothes and climbed into bed.

Her bed was freezing so she tightly curled up under her duvet. Once she had warmed up, she reached over to the drawer of the bedside table where she kept a photograph of her and her boyfriend hidden.

They were standing by the Bosphorus in Ortaköy; in the background were the 19th century neo-baroque Ottoman Mecidiye Mosque and the 20th century steel and concrete Bosphorus Bridge. They had purchased the Kodak disposable camera literally ten minutes before and had requested an elderly man who had been feeding the pigeons to take their picture.

That afternoon in Ortaköy, gazing at a blue yacht sailing in the Bosphorus, they had mused about going on a yacht journey from Istanbul all the way over to Cyprus, overnighting on the Greek islands. Some nights they would have to sleep in the cramped cabin. With no heating in the middle of the sea, with the waves rocking the boat, they would hug and be safe and warm.

They hadn't gone any further than kissing. She was growing increasingly curious about how it would feel if he touched her breasts. Presently, her nipples quivered. As one hand caressed her breast slowly but firmly, her other hand crept down to her thighs. She normally kept the pubic area shaven; it was a week ago that she had last shaved it and now her manicured nails scratched against the bristles. She traversed her labia and played with her clitoris for a while. Then gently Seher Aslan's finger wriggled in, towards her wetness, her softness.

Three months ago Seher had read the sexual health section of a daily tabloid where queries from readers were answered by a celebrity doctor with long white hair. A 14-year old girl from the south-eastern town of Mardin had written saying that she had never masturbated in her life and couldn't bear not masturbating any more. But she was scared of losing her virginity. What should she do?

The mild-mannered doctor began his response by protesting, 'Oh my daughter! Look at what is bothering you!' and then went on to explain that the membrane was deep in her, she should not be afraid, nothing would happen to her virginity. 'Come on, my daughter,' he jovially ended, 'masturbate regularly. 2-3 times a week.'

Seher is careful when she does this, for it thoroughly delights her, carries her away. Each time she does it she can detect a novel sense of pleasure taking shape in her. A pleasure which she is dangerously hungry for.

14

Soviet Binoculars

The evening before his next rendezvous with Mary Heather, Fehmi was quietly having supper with his family as usual. On the television the former Prime Minister, the first woman to hold the office, was complaining in her tender voice.

In 1996, of all parties, her centre-right True Path Party had formed a coalition government with the religious Welfare Party, with the post of the Prime Minister rotating. However, a year later, they were forced out of power by the military due to the anti-secular activities of the WP and the beautiful lady's hopes of regaining the top job were shattered. She was left with the sentiment that she had been robbed of the office. And currently, on top of that, she was facing corruption allegations, which she was aiming to quell with ridiculous arguments, claiming the source of her family's riches was cash and jewellery ·found in the bottom of a trunk in her mother's house after her death.

But Fehmi was hardly listening to the news; this evening he could not concern himself with how this woman had acquired her incredible wealth; she was

117

welcome to empty out the state coffers. Fehmi Aslan was dreamy. He was thinking about Mary Heather. Her healthy middle-aged body with a bit of weight... The flapping of her huge breasts when she was on top... Her nipples that were proportionally *just* the right size... Her feet which were what had attracted him to her initially... Her second toe that was a little longer than the big one... Her accent when she attempted to pronounce Turkish words... What she might be doing right at this moment. How his evenings would have been if he had been married to her... which was quite probable...

Mary Heather could have been his wife.

He and his brother had had the same start to life, the same parents, the same economic conditions, the same upbringing... Therefore, it could have been him who had been sent to America and married Mary Heather.

He turned to his wife.

The woman who was the mother of his daughters. The lady who cleaned the house, washed the dishes, cooked food. The person who took care of all of them. It was difficult to see any physical appeal. Her body was shapeless; her hands were rough; her skin pale; her clothes worn-out.

For many years now they had slept with their backs to each other: he on the left side of the bed, she on the right. This was not because they were enemies. On the contrary, they rarely quarrelled; Fehmi had cultivated the art of avoiding a confrontation and keeping himself to himself. He could not remember when exactly but it must have been around 1991 or 1992 that their sex life had ceased.

After the Soviet Union had collapsed, as they were once again free to travel abroad, the lure of capitalist money was too much to resist for some of the former communists. In the first phase, they brought their belongings with them to sell in the bazaars they set up in the cities around Turkey. Kitchen utensils, tools, cameras, army equipment, opera-glasses, Lenin busts – in short, nearly every re-saleable thing they possessed was on sale for unfixed prices.

Fehmi, like many other men in those days, frequently visited these markets. He wandered from one stall to the next, discussing the merits of the products with his fellow customers, and usually ended up buying something, convinced that he had landed a bargain. At home he paraded what he had purchased, praising its features and functionality, emphasizing how cheaply he had managed to scoop it up for. In the subsequent days, he searched for opportunities to point out the benefits of it, trying to offload it on his wife or daughters. When the weather was cold, he put on his Russian fur hat and, pulling the ear-flaps down, 'See, now it's warm,' he rejoiced. When neighbours came round he brought out a folding table for their coffee cups, saying, 'From the Russian Bazaar. Practical little table.'

However, more often than not these items eventually found their way into one of the heaps of Russian bargains growing in the various corners of the flat, with Tülin mumbling her discontent.

The binoculars were one of the exceptions to this.

When Fehmi arrived home excitedly that evening flaunting his latest buy, his wife laughed dismissively: 'Those are the only thing we were missing.' The girls took interest in them for a few days, but then gave up. They both were too girly for binoculars.

The first week Fehmi used them to scan the Bosphorus, the Golden Horn (into which the Byzantines threw their valuables during the Ottoman conquest in 1453), the Old City, the Blue Mosque (which with its six minarets rivalled the holiest mosques of Arabia), the Haghia Sophia (the church-mosque-museum, that big ship of history anchored in the heart of the Old City), the Rüstem Paşa Mosque (which was built by the great architect Sinan for the corrupt grand vizier Rüstem), the streets he was so familiar with… He managed to locate the seven hills Old Istanbul was built on and count the mosques within the city walls visible from the Galata flat. Gradually his interest shifted to birds. He was amazed by the geometrically perfect chevron formation in which they flew and how they seamlessly swapped positions, when the ones at the back took over from the tired ones in the front.

But what gratified him most was watching people.

From that corner apartment, he had a generous view of the piazza around the Genoese Galata Tower and the surrounding streets. He could spend hours gazing at the pedestrians, wondering where they were coming from, what their destinations were, judging their personalities from their appearances… And it was not long before his binoculars moved to the buildings, focusing on the lazy housewives lowering baskets from the windows for their grocery shopping; husbands slapping their wives; teenagers surreptitiously smoking cigarettes by half-open windows in their bedrooms; families crowded around a table after a tiring day gobbling their food as they glanced at the television.

Then, one day, in a flat on the other side of the square Fehmi detected something mysterious.

The curtains were always drawn but at times he could discern silhouettes of people moving. It was generally two people at a time: a man and a woman. Tracing their movements, he could tell they were undressing. Three days later he spotted fair-skinned ladies in high heels sashaying into this block. He was fascinated by this and, after work and at the weekends, he took to surveying this apartment.

When Tülin commented on how intently he was pursuing his new hobby, Fehmi ignored her. Tülin had no idea what he was looking at or what was going through his mind. She did not know that Fehmi Aslan was struggling with his conscience and that he was on the verge of reaching a decision that would set the tone for the rest of his life.

By then, Fehmi was already religiously more lax compared to the early years of their marriage. First, his observance of the daily prayers had become irregular. The physicality of *namaz*, that it had to be done five times a day, had turned into a burden. It was a chore rather than the soothing ritual it had been when he had first begun years ago. Unnoticed by anyone, initially he

121

skipped the morning prayers, and then sometimes he was too slothful to bother with the afternoon one. Eventually there were days when he went without praying at all.

Then, on his long walks, espying the people drinking in the *meyhanes* of Beyoğlu, witnessing how they were having a good time, he realised that he could not stop himself from questioning his resolve to abstain from alcohol any more. He was in his thirties and the feeling that life was slowly passing him by was overwhelming him. What harm was there in having a drink or two every now and then? Why not take a respite from everyday life?

It was interesting that at that time Fehmi intended to fit this urge in with his faith. He probed whether Islam really banned drinking alcohol. After all, most of those people who were imbibing at the *meyhanes* would consider themselves Muslim. Besides, there were the Sufis who believed in a metaphorical – as opposed to a literal – interpretation of the Koran. Sufis stressed the importance of an individual's one-to-one relationship with God and were not as strict about practicing the five pillars of Islam, some of them advocating inebriety as a way of getting closer to Allah.

But, as always with Fehmi, these were private reflections.

Things he didn't share with anyone. Things that he went to bed with. Things that he brooded over under the shower.

Around that period one day, on his customary stroll at

lunch break at work, as he was striving to switch off from the accounting work he had been doing, he ran into Hakan Yavuz, his friend from university. He had not gone far; he was on a street that he walked every day when he caught sight of Hakan coming from the opposite direction. He had not seen him since university – for more than ten years – and they both slowed down as they tried to recognise one another. Then there was the brief excitement, the brief smile, before a shadow crossed first Hakan's face, then Fehmi's.

Nevertheless, Hakan Yavuz proudly explained that he had been working at a nearby bank for the past year on a computer project and was going to move back to Ankara once it was finished. He had been specially dispatched here as one of the handful of experts in the country. He was married. His wife too had a career; she was soon to be the deputy headmistress of a primary school. And his son was top of his class.

'And you? Where do you work?' Hakan asked energetically.

'Working with my father. Still the same place…' Fehmi replied.

'Was it a textile business?'

'Yes, a clothing store…'

Frankly, there wasn't anything Fehmi could add to make it sound more positive.

Hakan received the message that Fehmi hadn't achieved much in life. He seemed to be dissatisfied. Then he changed the topic and inquired about his family.

'Two daughters,' Fehmi said.

'And your wife?'

'She is a housewife.'

Again his words hung in the air, before he thought of throwing the ball back at Hakan: 'Do you live in this area?'

'Somewhere in Fatih, in a two-bedroom rented flat,' Hakan replied before swiftly disclosing: 'But in Ankara we will buy a 140 square meter house with four bedrooms.'

An observer might have inferred that Fehmi had been domineered by Hakan. That Hakan Yavuz's superior accomplishments had silenced him. But then at a point when they could have wished goodbye, rather absurdly, 'Have you heard from Jale?' Fehmi found himself asking.

The urgency with which it came out made it so obvious this was what he had been targeting to unearth since the beginning of the conversation. That everything else they had talked about was insignificant.

In the early '80s, as a newlywed – when his memories of her were so fresh, it was impossible for Fehmi not to reminisce about Jale – he would imagine that she had been imprisoned in the course of the 1980 coup. The soldiers breaking into the flat, confiscating the literature on Lenin and taking Jale away in a moss green truck… Perhaps she would have even been tortured in prison. Yet, she wouldn't have given up politics. She would be dwelling in an ordinary apartment in a lower middle-class neighbourhood in an obscure Anatolian town, member of a minor communist party. She would still be with that boy who was quite a few years older than her

– the boy she was kissing in front of the cafeteria, the boy who bore an astonishing resemblance to him. And she still would have other naive boys in her life.

No, Hakan hadn't heard from Jale; he had lost touch with her after university. However, he had a vague recollection that she had stayed on at the university and had been aiming to be an academician. Anyhow, he was not sure. If he had any lingering resentment over Jale, Hakan Yavuz managed to hide this behind a blank expression.

'Let's meet again,' he said with renewed enthusiasm before they parted, and Fehmi agreed. They both knew that neither of them would call the other.

Two days after that encounter, on the Friday, Fehmi went to the Cumhuriyet Meyhanesi for the first time in more than a decade. Despite the long gap, the environment immediately felt so familiar it was as if he had been to this joint just last week. That night, as he was drinking *rakı*, he scanned the women at the other tables. At one point, his eyes settled on one whose nails were painted burgundy. She was tipsy and smoking stylishly. She would lean over to her male friend, whisper comments, kiss him, rest her head on his shoulder.

Fehmi Aslan could easily picture himself in that man's position.

He recalled the time he had returned from Ankara as a student, the months he had watched the river, the heavenly Rüstem Paşa Mosque, the floral tiles, and his notion of various versions of himself. The businessman, the family man, the adventurer, the womaniser, the careerist…

Of all those versions only one was alive.

The one that was a father of two, a conservative man. The one that lived in the neighbourhood he had grown up in. The one that had wasted his life working with his father in a clothing business.

And none of the other versions had ever come into being; they had never been realised.

The weight of having a family, the irrevocability of it all struck Fehmi in the face.

The children he had voluntarily begot would be his until the end of his life and he was not even thirty-five. He had experienced next to nothing so far. He could have married another woman – it didn't have to be Jale – and they could have dined at *meyhanes* such as this, sang songs, drank to their heart's content, then could have gone for a saunter along the Bosphorus in the early hours of the morning, celebrated the sunrise, the sunset, the summer, the winter, admired the mountains, the sea, the valleys… Or he could have remained single, given himself a chance to explore life…

His whole life could have been different.

Fehmi went home drunk that night and was barely able to climb into bed. When he woke up it was noon. He spent the entire day in his striped pyjamas, reading the week's *Milliyets*. Tülin was accustomed to Fehmi's occasional pensiveness but she had never seen him so dishevelled before. Fehmi acknowledged that he had had a *rakı* or two. However, he was not in the mood to talk, and Tülin judged it was best to leave him alone.

She just hoped that whatever it was, it would pass quickly.

By the time he detected the flat with drawn curtains, Fehmi had been frequenting the Cumhuriyet Meyhanesi for three months. Every other Friday he went there, sat on his own at the same table by the entrance, drank two glasses of *Yeni Rakı* with the same three plates of *meze* (feta cheese, stuffed vine leaves, aubergine salad), and returned home promptly at 10 o'clock. Once when Tülin inquired about his new habit, he responded melancholically, saying it helped him relax.

In the background, though, the concept of versions of himself was intriguing him more than ever. He was aware that he was stuck in one version. But also he was musing that the unrealised versions were part of him. They were somewhere in his being, dormant, waiting to be invoked. Perhaps, if he wanted to, he could even switch to one of those versions and then switch back. For instance, he could have a second version who entertained himself with women, and afterwards he would go home and be his conservative self.

He could maintain two versions of himself.

It was simply a matter of adapting to it.

As Fehmi drank and yearningly gazed at the other women and fantasized about the Russians in high heels, the versions were battling in him, the personalities clashing with each other.

Then one night an inspiration occurred to him.

Four days later, having reflected on it, Fehmi Aslan went to a travel agency in Taksim and booked a holiday in the Mediterranean.

It was Fehmi and Tülin's first holiday together.

Fehmi wasted no time. The day after they arrived in Antalya, he took out a black miniskirt from his suitcase and asked her to put it on.

'What is this?' Tülin mumbled. Never in her life had she worn such a tiny skirt. Even as a teenager she had not had the desire to.

'Don't put it on today,' Fehmi said, as she reached for her headscarf.

Tülin looked at him quizzically. But she hadn't yet understood what exactly was going on and her tone was half-mocking when she said, 'What do you mean? Shall I go out without it?'

'We are on holiday, let's have a change,' he replied.

Suddenly the air in the room turned ice-cold. It was utterly unexpected, completely baffling. Up to then Fehmi had at all times been conservative with regards to clothing. He was the one who had ordered her to wear a headscarf in the first place. And, after dozen or so years, headscarf was now firmly part of her being.

That day they ambled along the promenade, stopped at cafés, and Fehmi went as far as offering her a beer.

Then the next day he gave her a white bikini to wear to go for a swim. After the miniskirt this didn't shock Tülin. But it compounded her confusion. Why was Fehmi behaving like this? What exactly was he intending to achieve? When she tried again, 'Just relax and enjoy this break,' was all he said.

On the beach Tülin was too conscious of her body,

too timid.

'Try not to think about yourself,' Fehmi suggested. 'Everyone here is in swimsuits.'

Once in the sea, Tülin was more comfortable, and she decided she would remain in there to avoid lying in a scanty white bikini in front of all the men. But inevitably they came out. Fehmi was wishing to watch her sunbath, rub sun lotion on her just as the other men did to their wives. In the following days, Tülin was as nervous as on the first. And, finally, on the fourth day Fehmi conceded that she would not adapt and abandoned that part of his plan.

Even though they had not made love on a regular basis in the last 3-4 years, every night before they went to sleep Fehmi demanded sex. And it wasn't merely ordinary stuff. He entered her from behind, licked her, masturbated her, asked for oral stimulation. Even when they were younger Fehmi had not been as adventurous as this. By then Tülin was so disconcerted, suspecting that Fehmi had become unhinged, she could not reciprocate his enthusiasm. She just complied with his requests, waiting for him to finish. Like a lady who had lost her instinct for this ritual.

They stayed in Antalya for ten days. On the last day, Fehmi packed the bikini and miniskirts in his suitcase and told her to put on a headscarf before they left for the bus station.

Back in Istanbul life resumed its usual course. Intimidated and embarrassed, Tülin couldn't tell anyone about her time in the sunny Mediterranean. She had beheld a side of Fehmi that she hadn't had a clue about until then. She felt as vacuous as a teenager subjected to the whim of an incestuous father. She questioned herself about whether it was normal, whether other wives would have experienced similar things with their husbands.

As for Fehmi, literally his idea – his idea to involve Tülin in his alter-version – had flopped.

Two weeks after that trip, on a Sunday afternoon, Fehmi left home, saying he was going for a stroll. Since the days he had quit university, walking had been Fehmi's favourite pastime. Walking was his meditation and Tülin was used to him going out alone at any time of the day.

Rather than directly going over to the flat with the drawn curtains, Fehmi first sat on a bench near the Galata Tower and ate a *simit*. Then, to minimise the risk of being spotted, he turned up the collar of his jacket, marched down one hill and then back up another, and entered the street where the building was from the opposite end.

Going up the stairs, he came eye to eye with a housewife wearing frameless glasses. The woman gave him a contemptuous look. Fehmi paused and watched after her. Then he peered up the staircase. Years later it was the image of this staircase that would recur to him whenever he sought out the defining moment of his life. He decided then and there that there was no reason for him to be ashamed: the woman didn't know him, he didn't know the woman. That was the crux of the matter.

So Fehmi Aslan went up the stairs to the Russians in high heels. To heavenly delights, to the houris on earth.

**

Over the years Fehmi had trained himself to forget about the duality of his life, to pretend that his second version did not exist. On the surface he lived as he always did. Maybe he missed his prayers more often and drank once in a while but that was about it. There was no other visible difference. He had fluidly made the transition into having two versions of himself, to having a secret side. Only on the odd occasion did he slip up. As he had today, when he uncontrollably daydreamed about Mary Heather.

Now, at the dinner table, he noticed Seher was staring at him. Directly into his eyes. It lasted six or seven seconds. Longer than what would be considered negligible. But it was Seher who eventually turned her head away.

Fehmi didn't make anything of this exchange. Instead, he diverted his thoughts to Seher, to the way she had evolved in the last couple of months. Femininity was forcing its way through her body. Her voice was in that intermediate phase: somewhere between a girl's and a woman's. When she spoke, she exuded freshness and energy. Her nails were manicured and polished. She had been plucking her eyebrows – probably she had learned from her older sister who had started doing so recently.

He wondered what would become of Seher when she grew up.

**

In the morning, before leaving home, Fehmi reminded his wife to search the girls' bedroom for cigarettes. The previous night when they had gone to bed he had shared his suspicion with her that Merve had been smoking. Though he was a smoker himself, he was convinced he could smell cigarette smoke on her coat.

As for Seher, he had no evidence that she smoked but it was obvious how much she had matured, and it wouldn't surprise him if she had tried smoking too.

In any case, lately there was something about Seher's demeanour that worried him.

15

Behind the Curtains

Over the course of the 4-5 months following the fashion show, the performance of Renaissance Textile Company had proved Fehmi right. Their sales figures had consistently increased each month. They had several regular customers, mostly girls in their twenties, who were keen to frequently update their wardrobes with new models of headscarves and tighter clothes. Designers were knocking on their door to present their creations.

A month ago, two streets down, a store similar in nature to RTC had opened. They, too, had chosen an English name: *Star Textile*. Smart young women wearing headscarves was now a common sight on the streets of Istanbul. The wives of religious politicians were in the news more often with their extravagant shopping trips to Paris and Milan.

All in all, it seemed like this bourgeoisie religious class that had emerged in the early '90s was here to stay.

In this atmosphere Fehmi was excited by the potential of their business. In the long-term they could open another branch. They could even venture into

Nişantaşı, the secular upper-middle class district, which was home to some of Istanbul's best stores.

His short-term objective, however, was to establish the Renaissance brand by focusing on the clothing. And he was constantly seeking out new possibilities. Currently in the window there was a 1.78m mannequin dressed in a tunic, jeans, Converse shoes and a simple white headgear; in her hand was a tennis racket. Another dummy had a yellow headscarf that was knotted in the shape of a rose on one side.

And that day, sitting in the office at the back of RTC, pointing at an article in *Milliyet*, Fehmi was describing the *haşema* to his brother Rafet. The *haşema* was a swimsuit for conservative ladies designed to preserve their modesty – though it was an eye-catching costume to don on a beach amongst bikini-clad women in that it covered the legs, arms and head, and more than a bathing suit it resembled a tracksuit.

The article was about a famous singer who had been caught by the paparazzi sashaying out of the sea wearing one of these.

Not that long ago, probably about two years ago, this ginger-haired singer had been pictured sunbathing with her bikini top unfastened in Çeşme; at a few galas she had 'given a free-kick' in a super miniskirt; and normally on stage she would be in a generous décolleté dress. But, within the past year, she had first been filmed at the airport returning from Hajj pilgrimage (albeit carrying bottles of duty-free whiskies), then putting on a headscarf live on a television programme, and once creeping out of a Sheikh's villa.

In the photograph, the singer was in a light green *haşema* that had stuck to her body, revealing her fine curves. Given that it was windy, with not much sun, it was a strange day to pick for a swim. The newspaper maintained that the singer was disturbed by the presence of the cameras. Despite this, it included a quote from her, saying she *always* swam wearing a *haşema*.

Having lived away from Turkey for almost 20 years, Rafet was unaware of such a bathing suit. And when he eyed the picture of the singer with water dripping from her *haşema*, he couldn't stop himself from giggling. But, he agreed, yes, this costume was a better option for ladies who weren't willing to put on a normal swimsuit and instead swam in their clothes in secluded beaches. He was, however, doubtful of its commercial viability.

Would an ordinary person really swim in this thing?

'It's still rare,' Fehmi admitted. 'But chances are during a holiday in the Mediterranean you might come across one. On the same beach a lady in a bikini and a lady in a *haşema*! Go there this summer. Take your family, so they can see a different part of Turkey.'

Fehmi went on to relate that he had been down there with his wife around 7-8 years ago. The Mediterranean coast had developed tremendously since the '70s. Large holiday resorts were rising one after another. All-inclusive five-star establishments, vying to be the greatest. Extraordinary investments. English tourists, Germans, Scandinavians, Arabs... Hollywood stars were queuing up to go on 'blue tours' on luxury yachts.

And so many Persians! Persian ladies who couldn't go out without a headscarf in Iran were in bikinis on the beaches in Turkey – and how charming they were! Their white skin against their dark thick hair and large eyes...

More relevantly, Fehmi mentioned reading about a new resort being built by a religious businessman, which would have its own segregated beach – one side for women, one side for men. Unlike public beaches invaded by topless foreigners, it was envisioned that in this place most women would be in *haşemas*.

'So the real boom for *haşemas* might yet be a couple of years away,' Fehmi remarked. But they could order a small quantity to determine whether there was a market for them.

'What about a street fashion show?' Rafet wondered. 'Would it be doable, with the passers-by and all?'

'Why not?' Fehmi replied and pointed out that some stores had in the past successfully organised lingerie fashion events on the street. True, there would be more voyeurs, but he was certain there would be no trouble.

Shortly after this discussion, Fehmi rose to his feet, telling he had to deal with a problem his tenants had.

'What's the matter?' Rafet asked, unusually curious.

'The new heating system. It's not working. They have no hot water. So I will get somebody to look at it.'

**

Lying on the bed after they had made love for the third time, Mary Heather was musing that these meetings

136

with Fehmi were going to be a part of her routine from now on. It would be these 2-3 hour sessions that would keep her going; that would enable her to forget the misery of her life.

These afternoons were the result, the culmination, of everything else that had transpired in the past year.

Of Rafet moving them to Turkey against her wishes, of reneging on his promise to try it out in Turkey for a year, of not allowing them to go to America, of holding them captive in Turkey, of keeping her in the dark...

In the midst of that darkness, this was her sole pleasure. This was her revenge.

Mary Heather was savouring every moment in this flat but she was also finding Fehmi and his peculiarities amusing. He was again taking a shower. After each time they had sex, he conscientiously went to the bathroom. He spent a long time in there, obsessively rubbing himself clean, leaving her alone for a good half hour.

From what she had observed so far, a queer image of Fehmi was forming in her mind, an image that was impossible to reconcile with the Fehmi she knew previously.

Judging by his appearance, as a father of two daughters, neatly dressed in formal trousers and a plain shirt, she had imagined that he was a docile son who had done everything right in life, everything to the approval of his parents. That he had suppressed his individuality, that he had never taken risks, never done anything adventurous, never followed his dreams.

For example, when they sat and chatted after family

dinners, he was so keen to learn about America, it was obvious he was dying to visit it; and given his financial circumstances he could have easily travelled to America, yet he hadn't.

Or, as another example, when he stole a glance at her feet, he seemed so full of yearning, so hungry, so unfulfilled. So, in the middle of a serious conversation, when her mind drifted off to how he would be in bed, she would think that he had never sexually explored himself either, that he had endured a dull sex life with his wife in the early years of their marriage and had eventually become dormant.

Now she could clearly see that this was not the case.

Behind the façade of a family man who performed his prayers, behind the façade of a suppressed person, was an individual with a complex life. She could guess that there was more to Fehmi Aslan than merely these afternoons with her.

He must have used this apartment before. 'My mother doesn't come here anymore. It's painful for her to be alone in this place,' he had said at their first meeting. But she was curious about how he had begun to bring ladies here, since when he had had a second life, who the other women were.

There were other things as well that she was eager to discover.

For instance, what had he done with her black bra? Where did he keep it? What was in the drawers and wardrobes? She could ask him of course, but she was growing itchy to search through this flat, to see what it would reveal.

Mary Heather was walking around naked and had just opened the wardrobe to peek inside when she noticed it was approaching four o'clock. She didn't want to be late like last time; Ali would soon be back from school.

Next time she would start her investigation straight after Fehmi went into the shower.

**

Mary Heather was casually getting into the white Renault when her eyes caught a movement behind the curtains at Fehmi's flat further down the road. It occurred in less than a second: the moment she looked up, a shade crossed the narrow gap between the curtain and the wall, and then the curtains shook.

It drained the colour from Mary Heather's face. Her lightness evaporated. The gravity of what she had been doing suddenly became apparent.

She had strayed once in her life and was brought back in a second.

That was all it took: a shade shifting, the curtains fluttering. She wasn't even sure. Wasn't she too far for anyone to identify her from that apartment?

She sat still in the car watching for any other movements.

There was nothing.

Had she imagined it?

16

Crossing the Bridge

The next evening, shortly after they had eaten, Fehmi announced that he would like to speak to Seher. He asked Tülin, Merve and his mother to leave them alone in the living room.

Seher was puzzled; she had never been summoned like this before. It had been a week since Merve had told her about seeing her from an Ortaköy café and she had begun to believe that her sister would keep it to herself. Now, almost instantaneously, a doubt arose in her mind.

In the living room there were two couches with a coffee table in the middle. Father and daughter sat facing one another. Seher pulled down the sleeves of her grey Levi's jumper and, hands under chin, elbows on knees, she waited.

Earlier that day, reflecting on the matter, Fehmi had decided that this was a one-off incident and that he would deal with it calmly.

Seher listened as her father spoke in his typical righteous way about his responsibilities: earning money, bringing them up to be proper and respectable people, setting up a prosperous future for them. He told her that she was very young and that when people were young they could do things which they would regret later. It was there that the parent had to intervene. Then she heard him say that she shouldn't be going out with boys at her age; that she should concentrate on her education. And that she should not be wearing that miniskirt.

We have values, Fehmi Aslan added with a softer voice, when you grow up, you will understand that this is for your good.

As her father was lecturing her that day, Seher was wondering what she had in common with her family. Her father, who lived a boring life split between work and home, with no enjoyment whatsoever, only going out on his strolls. Her mother, who looked so provincial in her flowery clothes, she was ashamed of walking down the street with her. And her sister, who took religion to a more extreme level than all of them, covering up at her young age...

How could she introduce her boyfriend to these people in the future? These were not people she had selected. Why did she have to be burdened by them?

More than what her father had said, what disturbed Seher was how petty her sister had been. She and Merve had never been close; still, when it came to an issue such as this, she would have imagined their morals would be similar.

Had she whispered it to their mother, and she to their father?

The next morning Fehmi offered Seher a ride down the hill to the stop in Karaköy from where she caught the school bus. After the conversation the previous night, this was a step towards restoring their relationship. He had no idea where she hid the skirt or when she put it on. She presumably swapped at school; Tülin had assured him that Seher went out in her usual skirt every morning and he fully trusted his wife.

When they arrived, Seher got out of the car and walked over to the stop. But Fehmi didn't move. He waited in the grey Citroën saloon. Perhaps it was fatherly concern. Perhaps not.

Seher stood there in her bulky skirt, her white socks pulled up to her knees, as her friends appeared one by one. By then they were all used to seeing her in the other skirt, and each and every one of them eyed her up. Did Seher notice some boys giggling?

The episode must have been 7-8 minutes but it seemed like eternity with her father sitting there in the car watching. Seher wanted to disappear off the face of the earth. It was all so irritating.

That morning, when Seher did not turn up on time, Leyla phoned to check if she was sick. It was her mother Tülin who answered.

'Her father has taken her today,' she said. 'She must be at the bus stop by now.'

This had not happened before. But Leyla didn't dwell on it; she was annoyed that Seher had not bothered to inform her. To Mary Heather, she said: 'I don't know why, her mother didn't say.'

So she left home alone and Seher's ironed skirt remained on a hanger on the handle of the plywood wardrobe.

Leyla was one of the last to reach the stop. Spotting the grey car about ten meters away, 'What's going on? Why didn't you come?' she asked.

But Seher was too listless, too distant to reply. During the journey she chose to keep to herself, gazing out of the window. The eyes of the two boys in the seats next to theirs were on her, she knew.

When the bus was on the Bosphorus Bridge, crossing slowly over to the Anatolian side, she turned her head back in the direction of Ortaköy. On the near side was the Mecidiye Mosque; further on were the bench on which she sat with her boyfriend, the people in dark-coloured city clothes, the flock of fat seagulls foraging for food. She looked a little longer at the rundown apartment block on the other side of the square.

She had never really examined it before.

Being right by the Bosphorus, at one time it must have been one of the best residences in Istanbul. Yet, nowadays, it was a slum in the heart of the city. The faded yellow paint was peeling off. White underwear was hanging on the lines on one balcony. She imagined that the furniture in the flats were broken, tiles missing in the bathrooms, leak stains on the walls. There were probably burnt pots and dirty dishes in the sooty kitchens. The lift wouldn't be working, rubbish on the stairs. Mice and rats scampering freely in and out of the flats.

When would this building be renovated? What kind of people was it inhabited by? How did they earn their living? A moneyless poet maybe, who relentlessly pursued his dreams. Or a retired man who passed time reading the papers. Or maybe that happy transvestite they had once seen in Ortaköy.

That day the transvestite was wearing a white mini dress and high-heeled sandals. Her feet were as big as a basketball player's and her toenails were painted bright red. There was a man in a black leather jacket striding two paces behind her. He was considerably shorter than her and was telling her that she deserved to go to heaven. But the cross-dresser was showing no interest. Marching ahead, her head high: 'Why would I wish to go there?' she laughed airily. 'It's cold there.'

Seher smiled at this recollection and her own reflection in the window smiled back. Why a man would desire to dress as a woman was a question that often boggled her mind. Was it the result of a tragedy in his childhood – perhaps his alcoholic father stabbing his mother in front of his eyes because she had not cooked anything for supper as there was nothing left in the fridge? Or was it because of an anomaly in his DNA? And what did a transvestite and a man do together in private?

Meanwhile, the traffic had come to a halt. The sun was hot. Some people were listening to the radio news, some snoozing, some daydreaming. A few of her friends were smoking, telling each other their experiences and methods of hiding their habit from their parents. 'I have to smoke! I am addicted!' one was proclaiming. 'You try it too,' a boy was offering his cigarette to his girlfriend.

Seher's eyes focused on what was beyond her reflection. On the grey balustrades of the bridge.

The bridge that linked the East to the West in 1973.

She imagined herself standing by the edge, looking down 64 meters at the blue waters of the Bosphorus. At the tiny boats and ferries and the occasional Ukrainian freight vessels... She would clamber over, and throw herself down at once.

She wouldn't linger, hanging onto the railing, like that 31-year old unemployed man who was interviewed on television by the fat presenter Mazhar. She would jump at once. Without any hesitation. She would bring an end to all the nonsense of life.

Nobody had asked her whether she had been willing to enter this world but at least it was in her hands to terminate her existence.

How would falling feel? As some claim, would all her memories flash across her mind? Would she hit a ferry or a ship? And if she hit a ship, what would happen? Would they take her to Ukraine, to Odessa?

Then suddenly she was startled out of her reverie. The bus was moving again. Magically, as though it had never been blocked, the traffic was flowing. How could one make sense of the Istanbul traffic?

That day, Seher hardly spoke to anyone at school. Not even to her boyfriend. She told him she preferred to be alone. When he insisted, she promised she would tell him everything later. At breaks she sat in her desk, scribbling in her notebook.

She realised once again how much it was her physical appearance – her clothes, shoes, hair, body, face, hands, all combined – that made her who she was. And that even if one of those was not in order it affected her whole being, her morale, her relationship with other people, her outlook on life. It transformed her into a different person.

However controversial it sounded, appearance was of paramount importance.

**

In the evening when Mary Heather heard from Leyla what had transpired, why Seher had not turned up in the morning, she was exasperated.

Seher had been coming to their apartment to switch skirts for such a long time that it had blended into their everyday life and Mary Heather did not even give it a thought any more. Of course, she was aware from the very first days back in autumn that Fehmi didn't allow Seher to wear a short skirt or have a boyfriend... but, since then, with what had been going on between her and Fehmi, and all that she had gathered about him...

Nevertheless, Mary Heather was quick to regain her composure and tone down her response to Leyla. She had to avoid giving away anything by over-reacting to a matter involving Fehmi.

She didn't know, her daughter didn't know, whether Fehmi had found out that Seher had been keeping a skirt at their flat. And, if he had, what would his reaction to her be? Would she phone her again and, if he did, what was she supposed to say?

She had been mulling over whether to call him to tell about her suspicion that she had been spied on following their last rendezvous. But now how could she? At any rate, she couldn't meet him at her mother-in-law's flat again. Not after that scare. It was out of the question. She couldn't guess who the person behind the curtains was; it could have been any one of them residing in that flat. She could imagine how distressing it would be to face his family.

Suspicion was dreadfully consuming.

The last two days had been hell. She could learn to cope with reality one way or another but to be in the dark, to be uncertain was unbearable.

Why the heck had she parked the white Renault in front of the building? How stupid it was. Why did she commit such simple mistakes? … And, now, on top of that, the way Fehmi had dealt with Seher which she just couldn't accept…

17

Something in the Air

In the subsequent days Seher gradually settled into a new routine driven by her depressive mood. She reluctantly went to school in her long skirt. She was unsure whether Leyla's idea that she could change skirts at school would work – after all, she hadn't established what exactly her father had discovered. At school she was withdrawn, not speaking much, not going out at breaks. Now that she was used to the other skirt, her long one seemed even more incongruous.

Some days she just couldn't muster the energy to go to school and spent the entire day at home in bed. All she was wishing for was the school year to end quickly. And then finishing high school in two fast years and going to university in another city so she could be far away from her family. Sometimes she mused about moving to another school. In recent years private schools with conservative owners had opened; she often saw students from those schools in their ugly green skirts on the streets. She could transfer to one of those schools or to a state school and at least not feel an outsider.

In the evenings, straight after supper she locked herself in her bedroom and lay in bed doing absolutely nothing, not even thinking, not even daydreaming. Only staring at the blank wall. Later in the evening, when her anger subsided, it was of her boyfriend that she fantasized and she sought solace in masturbating to her heart's content under the duvet. Those private moments meant more to her now.

She cherished the freedom, the elation that masturbation provided her.

**

Observing the transition her sister was going through, Merve was worried that Seher might do something foolish.

The evening their father announced he would like to talk to Seher in private, she at once perceived what it would be about. And after he had spoken to Seher, she went into their bedroom where her younger sister had concealed herself under her duvet.

'What happened? What did he say?' she asked.

But Seher didn't wish to listen.

'Go away,' she howled. 'Leave me alone.'

'Look, whatever it was, I didn't tell anything, I swear.'

'OK, I don't want to talk about it. It doesn't matter.'

'But, Seher, it can't be like this. What can I do for you to believe me?'

'You can go away, for example.'

Merve was aware she was not sounding credible.

And maybe she never would.

Since that day Seher was ignoring her (and everyone else in the family), not speaking, not responding. Occasionally she gave her a scornful look and walked away.

**

Six days passed, seven days passed, but Fehmi didn't ring Mary Heather.

This was the longest gap so far.

Mary Heather was still debating, she had not yet made her mind up, whether to answer the phone or not. All the same, she yearned for him to call. She had to be the one to decide on the future of their clandestine meetings.

Every day Leyla was relating how dejected Seher was. As days went by and Fehmi didn't phone, Mary Heather grew more convinced that he had learned about Seher's skirt trips to their flat and that he was angry with her...

Or was it more straightforward than that: had the person behind the curtains confronted Fehmi and that was why he was refraining?

She had no clue, and she wasn't sure she wanted to find out. Mary Heather could smell something ominous in the air. Something was going to happen. She didn't know what. She could venture a guess, but her instinct told her that her guess would be incorrect, that events would unfold in a completely unforeseen way. It was an animal instinct, like a cat sensing an earthquake before human beings.

She was afraid.

It was a whole ten days later that Fehmi rang Mary Heather on her mobile phone.

It was afternoon and Mary Heather was alone at home at the time. She was standing by the large window which had a view of the Golden Horn joining the Bosphorus. Unusual for this season, the sky was overcast. Dark clouds were hovering above Istanbul. She could discern even from where she was that the sea was getting rougher.

This type of weather gave her the desire to be on her own, in the safety of indoors.

It wasn't until the fourth ring that Mary Heather arrived at a decision. At that instant, she wanted to remain where she was and watch the weather deteriorate. She wanted to hear the sky rumbling. She wanted to witness the lightning, listen to the rain pouring down, observe the rain hitting against the window. She didn't wish to speak to anyone. Not to Fehmi, not to another person. It was a feeling that was seemingly unconnected to Fehmi. But she interpreted it as a sign that she should not take this call. They couldn't go on with what they were doing.

It had to stop.

A couple of days later Fehmi tried again. This time Mary Heather was more certain. Without any hesitation she pressed the cancel button after the first ring. It was all over.

This was the end of her little adventure.

**

Then the following week something out of the ordinary occurred.

Rafet invited Fehmi and his family for dinner. It was probably the second time, at most the third, in the 7-8 months they had lived in this flat. Normally they went over to Fehmi's – and even that was rare lately.

The meal was disturbing from the beginning. Mary Heather had been hoping that whoever had seen her getting into the white Renault that afternoon would have opted to skip this gathering. But that was not the case: they all came.

There were drawn-out silences throughout the evening with the only sound being the clatter of knives and forks. Occasionally Rafet attempted to start a conversation. He described in detail the progress made on the house in the forest. 'We will move in a year's time, at the latest,' he said. 'You should buy a place out there too. It's beautiful, away from the city, it's so serene. You'll sleep like a baby there.'

The talk about the house, perhaps its relation to settling down, prompted Fehmi to ask, 'Will you go to America this summer?'

For a second Mary Heather loved Fehmi with all her heart for querying this. It brought back the memory of that Saturday afternoon at RTC on the crimson sofa, the day she had cried and he had held her hand. His gentleness and warmth. She stole a glance at him and then expectantly turned to Rafet, waiting to hear what he would say.

'That's the plan,' Rafet replied, stretching out his words. 'Let's see...'

Mary Heather wasn't going to allow this opportunity to pass by. 'We have to buy the tickets soon if we are to go,' she said.

Rafet coughed and reached over to the bowl of beans.

'Prices will shoot up otherwise,' Mary Heather stressed.

But Rafet was focused on his beans, so Fehmi inquired how much the tickets would cost and Mary Heather outlined what they had paid to fly to Turkey last summer.

And that was it. Nothing more was said on that subject.

That was the pattern of the dialogues that evening. Sentences hung in the air. Even those who had no reason to be uncomfortable – those who didn't have more information than the others with regards to the recent events – grew uncomfortable.

Mary Heather looked from one person to the other. It was impossible to tell who the one at the window that day was. Grandmother was quiet and miserable; she never spoke much anyway. Mary Heather was aware from what Leyla had told her that among the rest there was already tension over affairs concerning Seher.

What was obvious was that nothing could be the same after such a dinner.

When Rafet had invited them, Fehmi had been caught off guard. He had been aiming to avoid facing Mary

Heather in a family environment without understanding why she hadn't answered his phone calls. He considered producing an excuse at that moment; but that wouldn't have been the most natural response.

'Let me check with Tülin,' he said instead.

'Friday or Saturday, doesn't matter. You choose,' Rafet added. 'If this week isn't good, then next week.'

There was no way out of this. He had to select one of those days.

Fehmi wondered why Rafet was showing this hospitality right at this time. Then it occurred to him that Mary Heather could be behind this. But what could be her motive? Was it merely that she had ended the fling and was presently seeking to restore the situation to how it had been before? In any case, wouldn't it have been easier to meet in private first and talk it through?

'What's the problem?' Rafet asked at one point that evening, having followed Mary Heather into the kitchen. 'Why are you acting so strangely?'

She turned to him and at that instant a terrible suspicion, perhaps the truth, dawned on her.

It was Rafet!

It was Rafet who had been hiding behind the curtains that afternoon. Was there any chance of that? At that time of the day could Rafet have been at that flat? Or maybe whoever had espied her, had told Rafet? The hatred in his eyes as he stood there staring at her was so clear.

'Nothing,' she said. 'I'm just tired.'

Mary Heather's odd demeanour that evening was evident to everyone. And Rafet played the agreeable husband, striving to maintain a façade of normality. At the end, when they were leaving, 'Come again,' he said in an upbeat tone.

**

Apart from that one dinner, there was no variation in how Seher spent her evenings. She still retreated to her bedroom immediately after supper. She was smoking nearly every day and, guessing that her sister might notice that her cigarettes were missing, for the first time in her life she bought a packet of her own.

One night she smoked three in quick succession. She slipped out of her clothes at some stage and drew on her cigarette in front of the mirror in her white underwear. The window was open and the breeze was invading her body.

The week before her father had spoken to her she had tried on bikinis in a store in Akmerkez with Leyla, as they were intending to go to the swimming pool of one of the hotels. She had to postpone that now, of course, but one day definitely she would do it. She would travel to Bodrum or Çeşme, and lie under the sun until its rays penetrated every inch of her skin.

She unfastened her bra and let it drop and then she removed her panties. She didn't mind that her breasts were small, she was content with the size of her nipples, but she deemed her legs to be too thin. Later she tested with makeup and eventually took time over painting her toenails black. When coolness ceased to be refreshing, she shut the window and crawled under the duvet. That night, as she masturbated, her finger went in deeper and deeper.

She fell asleep shortly after.

When she woke up it was the early hours of the morning.

It was freezing, and where her thigh was, the sheet felt damp. She checked with her hand to ascertain she was not imagining. This was bizarre. Why was it wet? She sat up, pushing aside the duvet. With the moonlight coming through the window she could make out a dark patch on the sheet. She glanced at her sister's bed: she wasn't there; she must have slept on the divan in the living room.

She switched the bedside light on and climbed out of bed. Baffled, she quickly counted the days – no, it couldn't be that. Suddenly adrenalin rushed through her. Between her legs it was sticky. How on earth had this happened? Was this a nightmare? She jumped up and down as quietly as a marionette, dumbfounded, picking up things, putting them down.

What was she going to do now?

Mechanically, she pulled the sheet off the bed and folded it. Then she put it in an Adidas backpack, which she meticulously placed under the bed. Naked, she stood in the middle of the room.

There was nothing else she had to hide.

She opened the bedroom door. There was no noise; the flat smelled of sleep. It must have been 2 a.m. or 3 a.m. In the chest in the hallway she found a fresh sheet. She came back in and spread it over her bed. Then she cleaned herself and lay down, pulling the duvet over her head.

She was wide awake until dawn. She just couldn't stop herself from theorising where this might lead to. When the door opened, she had been sleeping for less than an hour. In her dream there were three stained sheets which she had first tied to one another and then to the balustrades of the balcony, and had escaped by sliding down; in the morning the neighbours had gathered in the street and were scrutinising the dangling sheets as if they were a piece of modern art.

Her eyes were stinging, her head was throbbing. She struggled to remember whether the whole thing had been real or not. She was naked, she realised.

It was her mother at the door, asking her to get up and prepare for school.

When she came for a second time, 'I'm not feeling well,' Seher said.

Her mother put her hand on her brow. 'Do you have a temperature?'

Seher stayed at home that day. She woke up around noon and had some *Knorr* tomato soup. In the afternoon she watched television, zapping impatiently. There was nothing interesting on during weekday afternoons – mostly silly entertainment programmes for housewives. On one channel was one of those male singers wearing full makeup but pretending to be straight; he was evading the questions about marriage as one woman in the studio was persistently offering her daughter to him.

In the ensuing days Seher's mood fluctuated between apprehensiveness and rebelliousness. Smoking was the only remedy, the only thing that eased her mind. Even at school in the toilet she smoked on a few occasions.

Then one day she decided for once and for all that she wasn't going to care. No one could prevent her from doing what she desired. The issue over the skirt was so unnecessary, so senseless, so bigoted. She accepted Leyla's suggestion that she switch skirts at school. On club afternoons once again she left school with her boyfriend and went to Ortaköy. To avoid being in a short skirt anywhere near the neighbourhood, she worked out an arrangement with Leyla for those days whereby she changed in the toilet at McDonald's and gave the skirt to her before taking the bus home.

With her boyfriend she was more adventurous. She kissed him more deeply and more passionately.

Life became as it had been in the past. It seemed possible that with time everything that had occurred in the last couple of months would be buried and forgotten. The rift between Seher and Merve. Seher's hatred for her family. Perhaps even what had transpired between Fehmi and Mary Heather would have no repercussions. That last dinner would fade from memory as an unexplained anomaly.

For the first time in weeks Seher was happy. One day, sitting in Yıldız Park, shielded by the bushes, she encouraged her boyfriend to touch her breasts. It was such a marvellous sensation that it made her think there was so much more, so much more that she could taste.

It was with that exuberance, feeling as free as a bird, like she never had, that she went home to find out later that evening that her father had disappeared.

18

The Headscarf Man

In the weeks after the dinner Fehmi did not see Mary Heather or call her again. He gradually reverted to his old customs. And on the day of his disappearance, he left home as usual in the morning to go to work but in the evening he failed to return.

When it was past supper time, Tülin tried his mobile phone. It was switched on but there was no answer. RTC had closed long ago and no one was picking up the telephone there either.

Following two unsuccessful attempts, when she was finally able to reach Rafet, he told her that Fehmi had left mid-afternoon saying he had a few matters to deal with.

'Did he tell you where he was going?'

'To the bank and something to do with his tenants. They hadn't paid the rent, I believe he said.'

Other than that he had no information.

Tülin waited for Fehmi until after midnight. In the past on a small number of occasions he had arrived home late; but generally he was careful to notify her in advance. His mobile phone was now switched off, or its battery had run out.

Mid-morning she rang work. There was no news. It was in the afternoon, when their anxiety rose to a level such that they were considering calling the police, that Grandmother broke her silence.

'Check my flat,' she suggested.

'What business would he have there?' Tülin said dismissively.

'You check it,' Grandmother replied without lifting her head.

There was no sense in this; it was the whim of a senile woman. But what else could they do?

Walking over to her grandmother's apartment, Seher spotted that her father's grey Citroën saloon was parked three buildings up the street. This was normal and it also meant that he had come back from work. Peering through the windows, she did not detect anything unusual in the car. She knew her father sometimes went for a stroll and sometimes to the coffeehouse by the Galata Tower. She also was aware that from time to time he went to Grandmother's flat to bring back things she had requested. How likely was it that something had happened during his brief time there?

She unlocked the door to the flat. Straight ahead of her was the kitchen. What she saw was puzzling: there was an empty two-litre Coca-Cola bottle, breadcrumbs and cutlery on the table.

Clearly someone had spent time here. Who could it have been? Was it her father or was there some other person inside? That possibility caused her stomach to churn. Inspecting the flat alone was not wise.

She left the front door open, securing it with a chair, in case she had to run out.

Next, she took a peek in the living room: everything seemed in order. Whatever it was it had to be down the corridor.

She was almost expecting the bedrooms to be turned upside down but the small one was not. She continued towards the master bedroom. The moment she was at an angle to see more of the room she froze: in her view was a foot in a blue stiletto.

She remained calm.

For a second, she thought of running back and grabbing a knife from the kitchen. Instead, she tiptoed further and there lying on the floor in a red bikini was her father Fehmi Aslan.

He had long before breathed his last.

Part 4

Mehmet Agop

19

At the Funeral

Police discovered no signs of struggle on Fehmi. There were four distinct marks on his back which had been inflicted with the whip that was found next to him. The theory was that, as he was being whipped, he had fallen and hit his forehead on the floor, and then he had been turned over. He had died instantly.

In a cardboard box by the wardrobe and scattered on the floor there were various women's garments, including miniskirts, lingerie, stockings, bikinis… and headscarves. Apart from that, the flat was tidy – nobody had gone through the drawers or cupboards; the valuables concealed under the sheets in the trunk had not been touched. Everything indicated that 41-year old Fehmi Aslan had been killed by people he was acquainted with or trusted, and most probably accidentally. The sole confusing fact was that his wallet was missing.

However, the police had no witnesses and no other clues. The downstairs neighbour was a tenant who had moved in two months ago. She was at work during weekdays, and, at the weekends, even though she could recall hearing noises from the flat, she had never seen the people going in there. The flat across belonged to an emigrant family who lived in Germany and was rarely occupied. The apartment building was on a busy and narrow street, and the few shops were further down the entrance. So the shopkeepers, too, were oblivious to who had been going in and out of that place.

It was only after she learned about the whip that Mary Heather's mind went to that very first afternoon in that flat, to the time she had stumbled upon a whip by the dusty shoes. She wasn't sure whether it had been there at her second visit. But from the third afternoon there was a fleeting image in her memory of the shoes in the corner and there was no whip; at that time she had been ambling around naked without a specific purpose, so she hadn't discerned that the whip was missing. Presently, she could swear that it hadn't been there. It must have been removed after their first meeting.

She had accepted Fehmi's explanation that the whip had been purchased by his father from the Russian Bazaar. Back then she had no reason to doubt that. And even if she had, what would she have done?

Despite the shocking news of his death, Mary Heather was not entirely surprised by what it revealed about Fehmi. During those three afternoons at her mother-in-law's flat there was something extreme in his intensity, his obsessiveness, his sense of gratification... She could easily picture Fehmi in a red bikini... the way he was hovering over her breasts, ogling her feet, asking for her black bra...

The recollection of the bra suddenly altered Mary Heather's thinking.

It was probably still in that flat, among all the women's clothing the police had unearthed. Plus, she had been spotted creeping out after their last rendezvous. Perhaps even someone from the public would eventually remember seeing a blonde foreign woman...

Almost instantaneously terror took hold of Mary Heather. It was amazing how rapidly it grew, to wrap its tentacles around her.

That night she couldn't sleep. She was full of fear, full of theories about what might happen. It was merely a matter of time before the police would question her. She was scared that she would collapse under pressure and everything would be blamed on her.

In the morning she couldn't summon the will to rise and start the day. Her brain was swarming with ideas. She would lock herself in, not go near the scene until the police were finished with the investigation. But if somehow they did link her, she had to be prepared. She had to invent a plausible story. How could she explain her size 38DD black lace bra being there? How could she prove her innocence?

The more she reflected on it, the more she was unable to feel innocent. The whole world was closing in on her, conspiring against her. She was overcome with guilt for a crime she hadn't committed.

Somehow she had to extricate herself from this tangle.

It was that morning when she was still huddled

beneath the blanket that the plan occurred to her. If she could have, she would have proceeded with it immediately. But it wouldn't have been reasonable to skip the funeral; she had to attend it and she had to be patient. Gradually the finer details took shape. By the time she was in front of the bathroom mirror, it was all sorted out in her head. She knew exactly what she was going to do.

She washed her face and reviewed it again and again.

The funeral service was at the Arab mosque – the mosque which Merve and Seher used to go to for the Koran course as little girls; the mosque which, like the Haghia Sophia, had once been a church before it was converted by the Ottomans; the mosque which was named after the Moorish refugees from Spain…

Wearing a black tulle headscarf, Mary Heather was present with Rafet and the children. It was the second time she was facing Fehmi's family after the day she had suspected somebody was behind the curtains. She still wasn't any closer to establishing which one of them it was. The exchange in the kitchen during the last extended family dinner had virtually convinced her that Rafet was aware of her afternoon excursions. But, contrary to her anticipations, in the subsequent days he had not brought up the topic.

One thing was certain, however: the hatred she had detected in his eyes. For she had caught that expression on a couple of other occasions. That expression was confirmation that their relationship would never restore to how it used to be, that the distance between them had grown to a level such that it was inconceivable to carry on. And even to Mary Heather the underlying causes of this breakdown were unclear. Just a year ago they had a relatively happy family life in America.

And now all that was gone.

A week after that dinner, one night Mary Heather had picked up her pillow and a tartan blanket, and had relocated to the couch in the living room. And Rafet hadn't objected, or even queried it; he had silently observed what had been taking place.

At the funeral Mary Heather was barely able to control her restlessness. She was going through the motions and was hoping for this formality to be over as quickly as possible. On her mind there was nothing but her plan; even fear had temporarily receded.

Then, at the moment she was least expecting, her mother-in-law didn't acknowledge her condolences. Nor did she look her in the face. It was a discreet snub and with the crowd around no one noticed this. It stunned Mary Heather. It woke her up at once. Quietly she shuffled along with the line of people.

20

And After

The day after the funeral, when Rafet arrived home in the evening he was greeted by an eerie silence. He walked past the children's bedroom: they were not there. The bathroom door was ajar. He peeked in; it was unoccupied. There was nobody in the kitchen either.

He entered the living room. No trace. It was unusual for them all to be out at this time of the day. The curtains were wide open. Through the large window, over the roofs of the other buildings, he could see the lights of the Anatolian side. Ferries were zigzagging across the Bosphorus, transporting the commuters back to their homes.

There was nothing out of the ordinary in the room. As always it was cluttered and untidy. Scattered here and there were newspapers, empty cups, a plate with a half-eaten apple on it. The leather pouffe had been pulled out of its corner. Pillows were piled at one end of the couch where Mary Heather had taken to sleeping lately. Dust had gathered on the copper articles. On the dining table were stacks of Mary Heather's teaching notes and books. How messy she was!

Rafet had paused, struggling to remember whether she had told him about going somewhere that day, when his eyes caught an open notepad with something scribbled on it.

He picked it up and read the note. For a long time, for maybe an hour or two, he could not be sure whether the note was meant for him or whether it belonged to some other context and the notebook had been left open randomly.

It sounded so unbelievable. But as the evening progressed and there was no sign of them showing up, the clouds of uncertainty gradually lifted.

Rafet spent much of the weekend sitting on the balcony. Every now and then he went back to the note. On Monday, he rang a senior employee at RTC to inform him that he was not going to come in for 2-3 days and left instructions in case of an emergency. He was not going to say anything about this development to his mother or Fehmi's family for a while. They were in mourning anyway. They didn't call him; so he didn't call them.

**

In the afternoon of the funeral Leyla stayed with her cousins, and Mary Heather allowed Ali to play with the kids in the neighbourhood – the funeral had hardly troubled him. Left alone, with a sudden determination, she scoured the whole flat. She found what she was searching for in the most probable location: in the drawer of the bedside table under other documents.

They hadn't been hidden.

Why had she assumed that they would have been?

Then she went to a travel agency in Taksim. Supplementing her savings from her teaching with her credit cards, she bought three tickets for the flight the very next day. They would have to switch planes three times (in Frankfurt, London and New York) but she didn't mind. Before Rafet and the children were back, she packed essential items in a few bags and took them round to Barbara's flat so that in the morning they could leave home empty-handed on a pretext without arousing suspicion. It was a precaution that turned out to be unnecessary, for Rafet was out when it was time to slip away.

'We quickly have to go to Barbara's,' Mary Heather told the children. 'I will explain everything later. We just have to go now.'

She hesitated between writing a note and not. She couldn't afford it to fail at this stage. Perhaps it was better not to risk it. Then that revengeful side of her prevailed and, just as they were walking out of the front door, she went back into the living room and, without the children seeing, she scribbled a note. She didn't tell them where they were going until they were safely in a yellow taxi heading for the Atatürk Airport.

On Tuesday, she rang Rafet to confirm they had arrived safely.

At the next phone conversation on the following Sunday she informed him that they would not be returning to Turkey. She was blunt; she did not give him a chance to respond. She had been gearing up to deliver this message over the last four days and the power in her voice was clear.

When he put the receiver down, Rafet went out on to the balcony. His immediate judgement was that Mary Heather had acted in haste and would repent. His concern (that appeared a little later) was how to conceal this from his mother, how to cover it up, if he had to. Up to then he had controlled all his life. He had made all the major decisions affecting his life. Now, for the first time, he was faced with a situation imposed on him, a situation he would have to learn to negotiate.

That same day Seher phoned and requested to speak to Leyla about meeting the next morning to catch the school bus. More than a week had passed since her father's death, the shock was over, and she was ready to resume school.

'They have gone to America,' Rafet said. 'They went last week. Mary Heather's mother was hospitalised, so they left urgently.' He did not have to say that he had not wanted to bother them with this the previous week.

Seher expressed her sorrow and asked when they would be coming back.

'It depends on her mother's condition. We don't know yet,' Rafet replied.

And for the next couple of weeks that was what he maintained to be the case.

The family were undeniably devastated by Fehmi's death but they chose not to dig into the details of it.

Publicly they went with the interpretation that the red bikini and blue stilettos had been forced onto Fehmi by his murderers whom they suspected to be intruders or debtors. Looking into the eyes of the people, this was the story they told.

They closed their ears to the muffled neighbourhood gossip about what might have really transpired in that bedroom. Inevitably, Tülin recalled the Mediterranean holiday they had been on years ago. Privately, very privately, she wondered whether those bizarre ten days, the black miniskirt, the white bikini, had any connection to this event. Or if the few days Fehmi had come home drunk had any relevance.

At any rate, she did not share these reflections with anyone.

Meanwhile, at the Galata coffeehouse, old men went on gravely debating The Rise of Political Islam. And the young men playing backgammon chuckled at them, continuing to doubt their dismal outlook on the future of the country.

About a month later, when it was apparent that Mary Heather was not going to budge, Rafet conceived the idea that he too could return to America and join his family there. He could tell his mother that they had not been able to adapt to life in Turkey. Next time he spoke to Mary Heather, when he mentioned this, she was taken aback and could not produce a sensible response. In her opinion they should have been talking about issues pertaining to the separation.

For a week or two Rafet was even excited at the prospect of going back to America. He was imagining himself cruising in a white Cadillac in the sunshine on the wide avenues. He considered the arrangements he would have to make, with the house that was under construction and RTC.

Surprisingly, Mary Heather did not decline his offer outright but she did make him understand her reluctance. She questioned what job he intended to do in America and what he would do with the business in Istanbul.

As the summer grew warmer, the phone calls became more sporadic. On weekend afternoons Rafet prepared himself fish and salad, and ate on the balcony, drinking *rakı*, appreciating the view of the Bosphorus. Some evenings he went out, always alone, drinking at the *meyhanes* and clubs in Beyoğlu.

Then one afternoon in August, watching the sunset from the balcony, he realised that actually he didn't desire to go back to America. He could not even bear the thought of re-entering the rat race there, dealing with workplace politics, being dependent on people he did not like. Here he had his own business, a degree of independence, a system that was functioning smoothly. Plus, he liked the simple aspects of everyday life in Istanbul, having his shoes polished on the street, buying a *simit*, doing his shopping at the grocery store on the same street as the apartment, the night life... He was still 39. He still had half a life ahead of him. Another lifestyle, another existence was feasible.

In September Rafet Aslan told his mother and Tülin that, for the sake of the children's schooling, they had mutually agreed that Mary Heather would stay in America whilst he took care of the business in Istanbul. His mother's indifference when he broke this news didn't escape Rafet's notice. He guessed it was because of her motherly instinct; she could sense he was keeping back the truth. As for the others, it was only then that their inklings of a problem hitherto undisclosed were confirmed. Even then their queries were vague. They accepted what they could deduce.

By the spring of the next year, a woman the family did not wholly approve of moved in with Rafet. There were rumours that she was a belly dancer or a third-rate singer. A woman deemed disreputable, in any case. Each time Tülin went over with the food she had cooked, Rafet ensured the woman was in the bedroom, out of sight before opening the door.

Leyla and Ali visited him in the summer. But, finding nothing else to do, they lay in front of the television at home for four weeks and left dissatisfied. Leyla came alone once more two years later. After that, their contact was solely through occasional telephone calls. It was remarkable how unceremoniously his relationship with them fizzled out.

Rafet and Mary Heather never officially divorced. He provided no financial support for the children's upbringing, nor did Mary Heather demand anything. She initially found a job helping immigrant students at a school and then managed to secure a proper teaching position and a mortgage on a house in the suburbs of Pittsburgh, PA, where she resided for the rest of her life. She shared the story of her clandestine afternoons only with one very close friend but never with her children. Sitting at her kitchen table overlooking the lawn, 'It was sweet of him to hold my hand,' she said, describing the Saturday afternoon in the office at the back of RTC.

Leyla married an American man, an engineer with a stable income, had two daughters, and lived an uneventful, quiet family life a block down from her mother's house.

Although academically successful, Ali never quite settled in life. He did charity work for several years in Africa, always yearning for something else, always feeling unfulfilled.

As for the house in the forest... After three years, still in an incomplete state, it was demolished overnight by the municipality when it emerged the construction company had not obtained the proper permissions. Rafet was left to battle it out in court with the builder who eventually fled the country, first by boat to Greece and then by plane to America.

A brown island in a green ocean was the sole outcome.

**

Merve continued with her studies (Elif passed her course but Merve refused to sit in for her again using her headscarf as a disguise), and, upon graduation, she worked at the women's arm of a religious political party. She frequently went into the slums of Istanbul where she distributed goods to poor families; particularly before elections these campaigns intensified. At 25 she married a devout young businessman who liked Italian suits and owned a Mercedes. He was willing for her to progress in her professional life. Citing differences in aspirations, they amicably divorced a year later.

On the eve of her 30th birthday Merve Aslan resolved to no longer wear a headscarf.

She still remained a Muslim and argued that, according to her research, in Islam covering one's head was not obligatory; that what was meant in the relevant verse was that a woman should not dress provocatively. She never married again and lived with her mother and grandmother in the Galata flat.

A whole month after her father's death Seher realised that her photograph with her boyfriend in Ortaköy which she kept in the drawer of the bedside table was missing. Only then did she understand how her parents had learned about her secrets. But it did not matter anymore: she reached a compromise with her mother and was allowed to put on a more reasonable skirt.

Following high school, for university she left Istanbul for Ankara to be far away from her family. There she met a boy who had a blue sports car. He was the son of a rich businessman. She dressed as she wished. She loved wearing miniskirts. She was not bothered any more that her legs were thin; she even preferred them that way.

Her boyfriend didn't care that she was not a virgin. He was curious, however, about how she had lost it. One day, lying naked in bed after they had made love, smoking a Marlboro, Seher recounted the incident to him.

'Were you scared?' he asked.

'Not at all,' Seher said, laughing lightly.

'Seriously?'

'Serious,' she replied.

Then she turned towards him. Caressing his chest, 'To tell the truth,' she said, 'for a while there was a worry at the back of my mind. A worry about whether it would affect anything in the future.'

Straight after university, at the age of 22, Seher married her boyfriend. Her contact with her family gradually reduced to rare spontaneous visits. She often wondered what it was that had caused her 41-year old father to wear a red bikini, what it was that had driven him to *compose* a second life at her grandmother's flat.

If there was one thing that Fehmi Aslan's life had taught her, it was that an ordinary-looking man could be as mysterious as that happy transvestite she had seen in Ortaköy.